A SPELL FOR EV

Can't get the kids to sleep? Try the **Bedtime Spell.**

Want to dance the night away? Whip up the **Wallflower to Wildflower Spell.**

Connect yourself with high society types by using the **Rasputin Spell.**

PLUS:

- Create floor washes for specific moods at home or work
- Concoct magical menus to serve at parties
- And much, much more!

The Supermarket Sorceress's *Enchanted Evenings*

Lexa Roséan

St. Martin's Paperbacks

THE SUPERMARKET SORCERESS'S ENCHANTED EVENINGS

Copyright © 1998 by St. Martin's Press.

Cover photograph by Herman Estévez.

ISBN: 0-312-96673-3

Printed in the United States of America

St. Martin's Paperbacks trade paperback edition / October 1998

St. Martin's Paperbacks are published by St. Martin's Press, 175 Fifth Avenue, New York, NY 10010.

10 9 8 7 6 5 4 3 2 1

for Jory

Froh, wie seine Sonnen fliegen
Durch des Himmels prächt'gen Plan,
Lauf, Bruder, *eure Bahn,*
Freudig, wie ein Held zum Siegen!
—Friedrich Schiller

NOTE TO READER

While the spells and enchantments which follow use commonly available ingredients, if you have any allergies or sensitivities to a particular ingredient, refrain from attempting that spell. Heed all warnings and instructions on the products you use.

CONTENTS

SECTION VII: NEEDLES AND PINS

SECTION VIII: SLEEP TIGHT

SECTION IX: SEASONS OF THE WITCH

SECTION X: HOME ALONE

SECTION XI: DEMONS OF THE NIGHT

SECTION XII: HARD AND HECTIC NIGHTS

SECTION XIII: INTIMATE EVENINGS/HOT AND HEAVY NIGHTS

INTRODUCTION

Welcome to *Enchanted Evenings*, the third in the series of *Supermarket Sorceress* books. Supermarket sorcery is based on the principle of kitchen magic and all spells require modern and easily obtainable ingredients as opposed to ancient and hard-to-find ingredients. The kitchen witch relies on the power of everyday items found around the household. This magic stems from the tradition of household worship as opposed to the more elaborate ceremonial magic which finds its roots in the traditions of the priest- and priestesshood of the ancient temples. In days of old, people usually had to make a long pilgrimage to visit the temple of their gods or goddesses. In between these visits, they developed a form of household worship that was more simplified than the rituals of the church or temple. If one believes that gods or goddesses can be found everywhere, there is no reason to believe that this simple and sincere form of worship is less effective than the intricate pageantry of the official sanctuaries. A simple altar with a dish of honey, pink candle, and a juicy red apple, designed atop your nightstand, is probably more likely to attract romance into your bedroom tonight than an offering left atop El-Kasr hill near the ruins of the Babylonian Ishtar Gate. Don't get me wrong—it would be more than enchanting to visit the ancient haunts of the Great Goddess—but it would be just as blessed to invite Her into your own home!

A word about ingredients: many people are conditioned to believe that magical ingredients should be spooky, old, or cryptic sounding. *Eye of newt* and *tongue of dog*—these are the things that spells are made of. How could something like *corn* possibly live up to the magical sounds of these ancient and cryptic ingredients? Well, first of all, if you want spooky, there have been several Hollywood horror movies made around the power of corn. As for old, corn was cultivated in pre-Columbian times. *Whole ears* is just as cryptic and creepy sounding as eye of newt and tongue of dog—which, by the way, are simply nicknames for common herbs. These herbs were easily available to medieval magicians, much the same way as corn is now easily available to the modern witch. Some of us are blessed enough to be able to pick it fresh from a field. Corn can also be found at your local market in the produce section when in season, otherwise you'll find it in the canned goods aisle.

All ingredients required in these spells can be found at the supermarket, gourmet deli, hardware store, or drugstore (fields of harvest and gathering for the modern witch). If a product cannot be found fresh or in season, use a canned or frozen product. Some spells should only be done at particular times of the year when the ingredients are in season (see *Section IX: Seasons of the Witch*). This is the way to work with nature. (See my intro in *The Supermarket Sorceress's Sexy Hexes* where I discuss the Kale.) However, witches are known as harvesters. There was method to our madness of going out and harvesting fresh herbs, drying them, and storing them for future spells. If you think you may need a sprig of pine needles in July, then pluck some off your Christmas tree in December. Put it in a jar and stash it. Fresh ingredients are always preferred, but in times of desperate need, use whatever you can get your hands on. Remember to follow directions, use intuition *and* common sense; *and* trust yourself and your magical intent.

Whether on the road or on the town, home alone or with loved ones or business associates, on holidays or any night of the week, you will find a spell to create a magical and enchanted evening. All spells contain ingredients packed with power according to both modern and ancient legends, customs, and lore. I encourage you to add these most important ingredients to each and every spell: *faith and confidence in yourself and your desires.* Also remember the witches' creed: *Do what ye will and ye harm none.*

There is a small sign in *ye olde occult shoppe** where I have worked for sixteen years. It reads: *All items sold as curios only.* This sign is posted to protect witches from those of little faith. The believers smile past the sign and buy the tools of their craft with perfect love and perfect trust. Remember, the most important magic is in you. These recipes serve as the sacred vessels to contain, carry, and channel your magickal will. Good luck and good magick. I wish you many enchanted evenings.

Blessed be✪

Lexa Roséan
△
aka Lady Venus ♀ ☆

*Enchantments in NYC

Acknowledgments

**Thanks for your information, inspiration, love,
and/or continual support:**

Kiwi Shoe Polish Company, Together Market, Seven Skirts, Lady Nina, Lady Brigid, Madeleine Olnek, Peter Conte, Hilda Ferrer, Paula Forester, Carol Bulzone, Enchantments, The Minoan Sisterhood, The Gansen Mishpokhe, Jennifer Enderlin, Sandra Martin, Lisa Hagen, Dean and Bishop, Shalomchen, Broad'y, and Tango, Jalup, Triangulo, Carina Möller, The N. A. B. Factory, Odl Bauer; Societé du Soir, Claire Bear, Garbo 180, Fatima.

On the Road

SPELL TO PREVENT ACCIDENTS

Ingredients:

Earl Grey tea bag

The Seals of Solomon are talismans used to invoke the spirits ruling the planets. They were designed in medieval times, but some people believe they were actually used by King Solomon. Each planet has five to seven seals that are used to bend the forces of nature in specific ways. The seal is traditionally drawn on parchment paper, etched into metal, or carved into a candle. The seal is then anointed with a specific oil or herb that corresponds to that spirit. Bergamot oil (found in Earl Grey tea) is used for the third seal of the moon, which prevents accidents that occur from sudden movement.

Use this seal to prevent accidents on the road or to prevent sudden attacks of any kind. I also find it useful at parties to avoid spills. Copy this seal onto an Earl Grey tea bag and carry or keep it around the house as a talisman. You can also put one in your car. If you are not artistically inclined, cut the seal out of this book and paste, staple, or tape it onto an Earl Grey tea bag. (Make sure you read what's on the flip side of this page before doing so.)

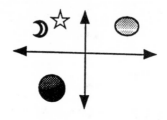

SHOW ME THE MAGIC

Ingredients:

head of lettuce
charcoal

One of my favorite movie scenes is in *The Tempest* when John Cassavettes causes a storm to begin at sea by taking off his glasses, holding them up to the sun, and saying: "Show me the magic!" I cannot show you how to do this magic but I do know a very effective spell to avoid sudden attacks by storms or wild animals.* This spell can be used to enchant an evening walk in the woods or an elegant night on the town. After all, you wouldn't want to ruin your *pas de soies*

---

*Do not use this spell if you are out for a wet and wanton night of savagery.
Check the **Wallflower to Wildflower Spell** instead.

in the rain, and who knows what kind of wild beasts are prowling around on the urban streets.

On a night when the moon is bright, go to the nearest body of water. Take a head of lettuce and hold it up to the light of the moon. Peel back its leaves until you reach the core. Gently place the leaves into the body of water and watch them float away. Lettuce is sacred to both the moon and Neptune, who are assigned to controlling the nature of water and storms. Whisper the date of your outdoor wedding or Sunday night barbecue into the wind. Ask the powers that be to show you the magic and keep any storms at bay. Lay a piece of charcoal on the ground. Charcoal contains carbon, which is sacred to Pan, god of the woods. Ask him to keep the wild beasts away in exchange for your offering.

ROAD MAP SPELL

Ingredients:

rutabaga

This spell is designed for people who get lost or space out a lot. It is quite useful for people who forget to show up at social, familial, or business engagements or for those who always show up late because they got lost or distracted on the way. You can also use the spell to avoid getting lost on the road and to get you home safely on unfamiliar roads.

If you are forgetful, rub the rutabaga across your forehead when you think you may have forgotten something important. Many omissions of memory can destroy an evening. (Forgetting to show up at your boss's birthday party. Forgetting to bring home the ice cream for your wife's dinner party. Showing up too late for the theater on a date.)

If you are in a car, bus, or subway and have lost your way, rub the rutabaga across a map or piece of paper with your destination written on it. Rub it in clockwise circular motions. Within a short period of time, the map will make sense to you and show you the way, or a sign or person will point you in the right direction.

Perhaps the highway is the least of your problems as you are lost on the road of life. Rubbing a rutabaga on the feet is said to give one better footing and direction in life.

Rutabagas are the queens of the root vegetables. A cousin to the turnip, the rutabaga is considered more powerful and is known for its magical properties of grounding. They never get lost, as they are always in touch with the earth. Rutabagas are sacred to the spirits of the four directions. Do not use a rutabaga if you are lost in an airplane. Their power is limited to the earth plane. You may, however, use a rutabaga to help navigate a safe landing.

SAFE CAR SPELL

Ingredients:

> **bay**
> **clove**
> **cinnamon**
> **Earl Grey tea**

Bay, clove, and cinnamon are all ruled by the sun as well as Mars. They are fiery herbs of protection and therefore are suited to protect vehicles run by engines. Bergamot, the main ingredient in Earl Grey tea, is ruled by the moon and is used to protect from sudden movement, e.g., your car being hit, towed, or jacked. Prepare a plastic zipper-lock bag chock full of bay leaves, cloves, cinnamon sticks, and Earl Grey tea. (Please empty the tea out of the tea bag and into the zipper bag, or use loose tea.) Place this bag in the glove compartment, trunk, or under the seat. Make sure it is hidden from plain sight. Often magic is not supposed to be shown out in the open. Many witches believe this takes power away from the spell. In the case of protecting a car, it is wise to hide the magic, as it will also affect the aura of the car and make it somewhat invisible or unlikely to attract attention.

ON THE TOWN

WALLFLOWER TO WILDFLOWER SPELL

Ingredients:

**vanilla
rosebuds or rose water
melon**

Are you tired of spending evenings standing demurely in dark corners, clutching empty dance cards, collecting matchbooks without phone numbers, and/or going home alone with no thrilling memories to mull over with your morning coffee? Try this spell before your next night on the town.

Draw a bath of warm water and add a handful of red and pink rosebuds or a cup of rose water, a quarter cup of vanilla extract or half a vanilla bean, and three tablespoons of juice from a ripe pink melon. Rose blended with vanilla is believed to summon boldness in those who are shy. Melon and rose are used to remove inhibitions and increase delight. Melon and vanilla are used for seduction and infuse sexuality and excitement into the auric field. Soak in the tub for at least seven minutes.

You can also perform this spell in the shower. After you have physically cleaned your body, stand in the shower, pour a bowl of this mixture over your head, and allow it to drip down the body (you may add water to the bowl, if the mixture is too dry). Do not rinse off. (If you have added enough water, the mixture will not be sticky.) Air dry or wrap in a towel when done. Then dress and go out for a night of wild fun.

ELLEN'S NIGHT OUT

Ingredients:

> **seedless grapes (red or purple)**
> **pomegranate seeds**
> **red candle**

This spell is designed for women who want to meet other women. I cannot stress the importance of using *seedless* grapes. A grape with seeds will attract men by the droves. You may, however, use the seeds of the pomegranate. The pomegranate is sacred to Diana or Artemis, huntress, ruler of the moon, and lesbian archetype goddess. It is also sacred to Hecate, queen of the witches, and goddess of women's mysteries.

Choose a table or shelf in your bedroom to create this altar. Cover with pink or lavender fabric and add any images you associate with female pleasure. Be as ornate or simple as you like.

Prepare a bowl of freshly washed red or purple *seedless* grapes and pomegranate seeds. Stand in the shower or tub and rub the whole body with these sacred fruits. Rinse off with water only. You should be physically clean before doing this. To finish and seal the ritual, eat seven grapes and hold one pomegranate seed under the tongue for three minutes. Remove from your mouth and place on your altar next to a burning red candle. If you are interested in exploring the sexual underworld with women, swallow the pomegranate seed. This is how Persephone made her way into the underworld according to Greek legend. If you are not ready for a heavy experience, sexual or otherwise, do not eat the pomegranate seed.

Note: The more seeds you eat, the wilder the night.

GLAM SPELL

Ingredients:

> **linden tea**
> **apples or fresh-pressed apple cider**
> **guava or guava juice**

The linden tree is known for its longevity, and the tea has been used for centuries in immortality spells. The Greek gods and goddesses are said to have eaten apples to make themselves immortal. The guava is a fruit sacred to Venus, and its pulpy, juicy center evokes the image of a wet and fertile womb. In the Philippines, guava is eaten for purification after attending funerals and also to invoke the image of rebirth.

Work this spell on a new moon to rejuvenate yourself and invoke a youthful appearance. Prepare a paste from apple and guava pulp and add linden tea after it has brewed and cooled. Use as a face or body mask. Leave on for ten minutes and then wash off with lukewarm water. You can also drink a potion of warm linden tea with fresh-pressed apple juice or cider and guava juice.

A personal secret—eat truffles to maintain a constant peak. The expensive fungus is hard to find but should be eaten on a full moon to heighten your sense of style and make you more glamourous.

COUCH POTATO SPELL

Ingredients:

> **mustard seed**
> **dried hot chili pepper**
> **coffee beans**

Are you (or is your mate) a chronic couch potato? Do you find it hard to get out of the house at night? Place these items underneath the couch to make you feel antsy and to get you up and out. You can also make a pouch and place it behind the television. The combination of chili pepper and coffee creates anxiety and restlessness. Mustard seed, ruled by Mars, gives energy, drive, and motivation. You can also add a little mustard seed powder inside your shoes or rub the powder on your feet to give you that get-up-and-go feeling.

FABULOUS WARDROBE SPELL

Ingredients:

> **thread (white and green)**
> **jasmine rice or jasmine tea**
> **lotus- or honeycomb-shaped cereal**

a book (or fashion magazine)
a pen

Are you fishing for a new wardrobe? Thread (cotton) is ruled by the moon and was used in medieval days for fishing magic. Thread is also a realistic representation of clothing. Witches use thread to weave wishes.

Jasmine is sacred to Laksmi, the Hindu goddess of beauty and opulence. There is a saying: "Whatever Laksmi wants, Laksmi gets." There is another saying: "It is most profitable to dedicate yourself to Laksmi." Laksmi's favorite color is green. The incantation for Laksmi is "Om Kamala Vaseene Kamala Maha Laksmi raja-may dayhey dayhey varaday swaha." She likes to hear it chanted on the full moon. Offer Laksmi a bowl of jasmine rice or jasmine tea and chant to her as you visualize a fabulous new wardrobe coming into your possession. Wrap a spool of green thread clockwise around the cup of tea or bowl of rice as you chant.

Unless your taste runs toward the ostentatious, I also recommend you offer something to Sarasvati, the sister of Laksmi. She is the goddess of intelligence, craftsmanship, poetry, art, and style. They say that petitioning Laksmi alone will bring you dross or garishness. A story is told of a man who petitioned Laksmi and received an unmined diamond field. The man's wife invoked Sarasvati and was led to a brilliant diamond cutter who created a priceless multifaceted gem. Laksmi leads to Versace. Sarasvati walks the Jil Saunder runway.

Sarasvati loves the lotus. Her favorite mantras are "Hrim Hrim" and "Aim Aim."* She also loves books and pens. She doesn't like you to eat meat or fish on the thirteenth day of the month either. It is written that if you chant her mantra twenty-one times on the thirteenth day of the month, you will receive what you wish.

*Vibrate the *m*'s on the lips when you chant this.

On the thirteenth night of the month,** place another bowl on the altar. Offer Sarasvati some lotus- or honeycomb-shaped cereal. Chant her mantra and wrap a spool of white thread clockwise around the bowl. Sit down with a book and pen and write down the kind of clothes you would like. (If you are a designer, this would be the time to sketch new designs, for Sarasvati will inspire you.) You can also leaf through fashion magazines and cut out the clothes you like. Pile them on top of the bowl of jasmine and the bowl of lotus upon the altar.

Leave the altar intact until you see some manifestation. You may also take a pinch of jasmine rice and a pinch of cereal from the bowl and sew them up in a silk pouch with green and white thread. Carry this talisman for luck when you go shopping.†

**A full moon falling on the 13th of the month is obviously the most auspicious time to work this spell.

†Believe me, shopping is not the only way to make this spell manifest. You may be given an entirely new wardrobe. You might find incredible deals on designer clothes. Perhaps you'll be inspired to sew again. The goddess will fulfill each person's individual needs according to his or her sphere of availability.

That's Entertainment

ARRABAL'S SPELL

Ingredients:

 cafe au lait
 croissant
 assorted sushi
 teddy bear

On the top floor of a midtown Manhattan office building, there is an extraordinary teddy bear factory. During the day, thousands of bears, poodles, and rabbits are designed, sewn, and shipped all around the world. But as soon as the stars come out at night, the top floor of the factory transforms, and a dozen or two lucky guests are invited to a sky-lit room to dance the tango underneath the Manhattan stars. If you are even luckier, the hostess will give you the tour. Downstairs, there is a huge room filled with sewing machines and rows and rows of multicolored spools of thread and ribbons. This is where the teddy bears are sewn, and also where the proprietress designs her own clothes. In another room hang rows and rows of uncut bearskins (fake fur, of course), and boxes from ceiling to floor containing teddy bear eyes, teddy bear noses, poodle tails, rabbit whiskers, and other assorted synthetic parts. Couples whirl counterclockwise round the top floor, and at some point after midnight and several bottles of wine—the teddy bears come to life. People, bear, poodle, and rabbit all merge into one. It is surreal and wonderful. Albeart Einstein even asked me for a waltz. I kid you not!

I began to observe the woman who made these evenings possible, trying to discover where she drew her powers of enchantment from. Arrabal is by far the most mesmerizing woman I know in New York City—make that Paris and Buenos Aires as well! Arrabal is a fierce warrior in the daylight. She runs a massive multimillion-dollar corporation from two continents with the wrath of Genghis Khan. She speaks seven languages perfectly and everyone is always wondering where Arrabal is from. Could it be Paris, Berlin, Buenos Aires, Monaco? I happen to know she was born and raised in upstate New York, but her charm and world-liness make Arrabal at home almost anywhere. Wherever Arrabal is, she possesses the place. She glows in the Palais Royale and glistens in the back of a pickup truck on the interstate. You cannot take Arrabal out of her element, as she thrives in all elements.

Arrabal has this amazing ability to care and love and be aware of all present. She treats her guests like foreign dignitaries and family all in the same breath. Everyone loves her. Even her enemies respect her enough to leave a room when she enters. For Arrabal is fearless and can pack a mean punch. She has had many a brawl at her parties. Believe me, they are just as entertaining as the dance. She is a wild thing and loves to take center stage, yet she never hogs the limelight. Truly a magical quality to possess.

The most remarkable thing about Arrabal is the way she dances. Men and women have been known to get on their hands and knees and beg Arrabal to dance. At a certain point in these evenings, Arrabal selects a CD and playfully moves to the center of the room. All the guests stand in a circle to watch her fabulous footwork. Arrabal can move swifter than the wind, quicker than the eye. Her lithe feet seem to glide across the sky. Her dance makes one laugh and cry. She is awe-inspiring, and I have heard several people say that her dance makes them feel glad to be alive. I remember one night feeling not only glad to be alive, but unafraid to die, for in Arrabal's feet I caught a glimpse of the magnificent world to come.

Arrabal drinks cafe au lait and eats a croissant every morning for breakfast. Croissants are ruled by the moon. They represent glamour, enchantment, and wishes. The croissant holds the magical shape of the horns of Isis: "the eternal divinity, who are one and all things."* Devotees of Isis would hold cornucopian feasts and were initiated into the mysteries of the sacred dance. Coffee is ruled by Mars, who endows us with our passion in life. It is also sacred to Chango, the Cuban/African Orisha who rules business acumen and *iwa-pêlê*—good character. Now, these two ingredients by themselves do not a consummate enchantress make, but Arrabal does not live by breakfast alone. Her favorite food is sushi. Lots of sushi. Sushi, or raw fish, is ruled by the sign of Pisces. Pisces of course rules the feet. The combination of coffee and sushi gives enormous amounts of energy to the feet. Mixing Mars energy with Pisces energy gives one all the subtleties of a nuclear-armed submarine. Quite dangerous. People with Mars in Pisces are also charmers: vulnerable, sexy, and very intuitive. Adding the croissants, or lunar energy, to this brew creates wonderful illusions and glamour and could possibly inspire worship.

I believe Arrabal's fourth magical ingredient is all the teddy bears she surrounds herself with. Bears are fiercely loyal, and Arrabal has the most loyal and devoted

---

*Ancient Latin inscription. Source: Harry Wedeck and Wade Baskin, *Dictionary of Pagan Religions* (New Jersey: Citadel Press, 1973).

group of friends. We would do anything for her. The creation of the teddy bear was inspired by President Teddy Roosevelt's refusal to shoot a poor helpless bear cub that had been trapped for him to hunt. Arrabal would never attack a helpless thing, but gods help any self-possessing beast that tries to cross her path. Do not cross Arrabal's path. During the day she is a street fighter, a rough rider just like Uncle Theodore. Yet at night she transforms into a gentle gliding teddy bear whom everyone loves to hold in their hearts.

PERFECT PARTY SPELL

Ingredients:

> **basil**
> **cardamom**
> **sunflowers**
> **yellow, pink, white, and red carnations**
> **cat toys with bells inside them**

Bast is the Egyptian cat goddess. She rules and protects the home. She is also known as the party animal goddess because her festivals were always celebrated with the greatest of mirth. This spell is to invoke Bast energy into any space where you are planning to throw a party. Begin by preparing a floor wash with warm water, crushed basil, and cardamom. These herbs are sacred to Bast. Wash the entire floor with this mixture. If the room is carpeted, prepare the mixture in a spray bottle and mist the entire room moving in a clockwise direction. In traditional witches' incense blends, basil and cardamom are used for both attraction and success.

Decorate the room with fresh sunflowers and carnations of all colors. Use pink predominantly if the party is for flirting. Use red for energy and interaction, or to create serious romantic overtones. Yellow is for success and happiness, and white is used to keep the energy clear in the space. I recommend combining all colors to create all kinds of possibilities. The carnation and the sunflower are both used to summon Bast.

About an hour before the party begins, circle around the entire space clockwise with a cat toy in each hand. Make sure you use a cat toy with a bell inside. My personal favorites are the multicolored plastic balls with little bells inside. Run around the space shaking the toys to ring the bells, and call out all the attributes you wish the party to possess. When you have finished, chant: "Mau, Mau, Mau, Bless my party with this spell."

Mau is the Egyptian word for cat and one of the names of Bast. It sounds like the meow of a cat and is also a root word for Mother. Bast is one of the triple Mother goddesses. Her aspect as Bast is very playful, like that of a kitten. Her aspect as Hathor is protective and nurturing. Hathor's presence could be invoked for a baby shower. Her third aspect is that of Sekhmet. Do not invoke the Sekhmet aspect unless you plan to have a war party. Sekhmet is the avenger, the warrior. She also has an aversion to men. Under some circumstances it may be appropriate to welcome her in. A radical feminist political rally would gain by her presence.

Once you have rung the bells and welcomed Bast in, relax and welcome in your guests. The party will be a success.

ROSEMARY'S BABY SPELL

Ingredients:

goat meat or goat's milk

Human sacrifice was quite common in the ancient world, even amongst kings. Agamemnon sacrificed his beloved daughter Iphigenia to win the Trojan War. Abraham was asked to sacrifice Isaac and then at the last moment God stopped him. Yet years later, God himself sacrificed his only begotten Son, Jesus Christ, to atone for the sins of mankind.

I cannot speak with absolute authority on the needs and requirements of God, but I can tell you with absolute certainty that that horny god of the witches, erroneously referred to by Church fathers as the Devil, does not want to eat your children (or beget them with you either). So, why sell your soul or the soul of your child when you can bribe your way into the horny god's heart? He would much rather receive a nice plate of goat meat smothered in goat milk. I don't know about where you live, but in my neighborhood you can get goat meat for 97¢ a pound.

The goat is ruled by Saturn or Capricorn; it is associated with power and material attainment. The goat is sacred to Pan, the god of the witches. Pan is the god of mystery and wonder, and grants the wildest of requests. To be completely politically correct, you should probably raise goats on a hillside or mountain top to please Pan. Or you could go to a petting zoo and feed a baby goat. Whisper your request in his ear as he nibbles at the seeds stuck between your fingers. But know that the smell of goat in any form, dead or alive, will attract this powerful god of nature. He can create storms, bend trees, and turn the fate of any man or woman.

This spell is used to bend the fates and improve your position on the financial or material plane. It is especially useful for actors who need exposure. Perhaps you are only an understudy for a big star and need an opportunity to strut your stuff. Maybe you already have a gig but need a good review or a certain casting agent to show up and see you. Perhaps you are an executive and are giving an evening presentation of vital importance. If you cannot hold court with a live goat, simmer a stew of goat meat and goat milk. Once cooked, transfer it to a bowl or plate and leave it under a tree or atop a hill at midnight as an offering to Pan, the goat-foot god.

BIRTHDAY MAGIC

Ingredients:

> **birthday candles**
> **olive oil**
> **assorted cakes**

The modern traditions of birthday celebrations find their roots in Egypt and Greece. The first birthdays were celebrated by the ancient pharaohs. The birthday cake and birthday candles originated with the celebration of the moon goddess Artemis. A round cake of flour and honey was fashioned to symbolize the full moon, and candles were placed on top of the cake to represent the moonlight. The custom of blowing out the candles and making a secret wish originates from the German celebration of the Kinderfest, a holiday honoring the birthdays of children.

Candles have long been used in spell craft to direct energy, purpose, and will.

Here are some magical tips to enhance the old traditions and infuse them with additional bewitching intent.

There is another custom of placing the same number of candles on the cake as the age of the birthday person, plus one extra candle for life or good luck. This extra candle is considered the magic or wish candle. Anoint this extra candle with olive oil to give extra life and good health to the birthday boy or girl. The color of candles is also significant. Pink candles will bring a year of new romance; red stands for deep abiding love or physical energy. Yellow is for happiness and/or fame; green brings prosperity and/or healing; orange represents success and creativity. White is for spiritual cleansing and blue is for peace and protection. You can use an assortment of all these colors to bestow a rainbow of blessings upon the celebrant. However, choose the color of the wish candle* based upon the priorities of the birthday boy or girl, as this color and what it represents will become the dominant theme of his or her year. When the candles are lit, and the cake is presented, all lights in the house should be dimmed. This reinforces the image of the goddess and the light of her full moon shining in the night sky. It is also traditional to light the candles and then lift and carry the cake toward the celebrant. This is representational of the moon moving across the heavens. Whether the birthday falls on a full moon or not, this image will empower the birthday wish and help it to come true.

Tradition calls for a secret wish to be made and then all the candles to be blown out in one breath. Witches believe that a magic candle should be burned until it extinguishes itself. This custom arose because often wishes will be inscribed on a candle, and you want to make sure that all the writing on the wax melts down so that your prayer will be fully answered. Some witches will never blow out a candle

*The wish candle should be placed in the center of the cake.

(or even pinch it out) once it has been lit. Others will put the candle on and off as desired, but will never get rid of the candle until it has completely finished burning. To make sure your birthday wish completely manifests, once you have made the wish and blown out the candles remove the candles from the cake, secure them on a piece of foil or a plate, relight them, and let them burn down completely.

Types of cakes are also significant. A pineapple filling will bring prosperity. Cherry filling brings self confidence. A chocolate and strawberry cake will bring sexual prowess and romantic intrigue. Carrot cake bestows sharper vision, focus, and insight. Coconut or lemon cake removes obstacles in life. Whether you are celebrating your own birthday or that of a loved one, incorporate these additional rituals to magically affect the whole year.

CHARMERS

FIRST IMPRESSION SPELL

Ingredients:

> vanilla
> oranges
> pumpkin seeds
> rainwater
> a hand fan

This spell will help you to create a positive first impression. Oranges and pumpkin seeds are both sacred to Oshun, the goddess of love and flattery. The combination of the two foods promotes success and immediate likability. Rainwater, especially when collected during a thunderstorm, can illicit a dramatic aura around your persona. Vanilla scent combined with a fan is used for seduction and charisma.

Before you go out, ingest five orange slices and five pumpkin seeds. Add five drops of vanilla extract or scent to the collected rainwater. Dip the edges of the fan in the water and flap or brush the fan across your entire body. Start at the midsection, work your way up the body, then return to the midsection and work your way down. You may dip the fan in the water as many times as you wish. The fan should just lightly touch the skin or not at all. When you are done, snap the fan shut with a flair. You are now ready to make a lasting first impression.

RASPUTIN SPELL

Ingredients:

squash

Rasputin was a social climber of the highest order. Born and raised in poverty, he rose through the ranks and attached himself to the royal Russian family. The Tsaritsa Alexandra would not dare make a move without his advice. Eating squash can help you climb to great heights socially in addition to enhancing your psychic abilities.

Squash was considered a very spiritual plant by the early Native Americans. Squash blossom necklaces were worn by shamans and healers. To observe squash growing in a garden, though, one gets a more complete picture. It grows like a benevolent ruler; its leaves, as large as elephant ears, spread in luxury and grandeur up the picket fence providing shade against the cruel August sun. It has a calming quality to its gregarious nature. However, upon closer inspection, you will notice that the vines produce little spindly creepers that grab hold of the earth and spiral down to produce new shoots. These little spiral outgrowths also wrap themselves around other plants and choke the more delicate summer flowers to help the squash expand. I have actually observed a wisteria and several impatiens being completely uprooted by the wide grinning squash.

Eat squash constantly in all its varieties if you aspire to climb to great social heights and squash all those on ground level as you ascend.

VAMPIRE SPELL

Ingredients:

> **beets**
> **steak tartare**
> **garlic**
> **tabasco sauce**
> **pimientos**
> **juicy tomatoes**
> **red wine**

If you are out for blood, eat beets and steak tartare. Eating meat is said to help you hold your ground. Beets give you longevity and legend says immortality as well. All bleeding red foods represent strength and voracity. They also hold commanding, charismatic, and hypnotic qualities, because they are ruled by the sign of Scorpio.

This blend is great to eat when you feel constantly drained. To ward off psychic vampires add garlic.

To win at sporting competitions, legal battles, or verbal debates add the Martian element of tabasco sauce and pimientos.

If you are interested in increasing your sexual allure, add a juicy steak tomato. Juicy tomatoes represent eroticism.

For political power, add a solar ingredient such as red wine.

JEZEBEL AND GIGOLO SPELL

Ingredients:

> **lime**
> **vanilla**
> **sage**
> **cinnamon sugar**
> **nutmeg**

Sage is sacred to Jupiter, that sagacious big spender. Combined with lime, it commands generosity. Vanilla is added as a sexual tease. To induce men or women to spend money on you, dust your hands with a powder made of crushed vanilla bean, sage, and four drops of lime juice.

To attract a sugar momma or poppa add powdered cinnamon sugar to the blend.

If you need to tighten your belt or ward off money-grubbing social climbers, fill your right shoe with a pinch of powdered sage, vanilla bean, and lime peel. Add a touch of nutmeg powder so that you can see them coming.

DO WHAT YOU WANT WITH ME SPELLS

Wouldn't it be nice to have that workaholic of a boy/girlfriend come home early one night to fulfill your every fantasy? Would you like that girl/boyfriend who sleeps till noon to get up at the crack of dawn and bend over backwards to please you? Maybe you want to kick up your feet at work, bark out some orders, and let somebody else sweat while you enjoy the easy life? These spells are designed to make others do your bidding. The ingredients are found in traditional witches' blends known as controlling and compelling powders.

Commanding Love Powder

Ingredients:

cinnamon powder
allspice
clove
rose
clover honey
lime
bay

Cinnamon, allspice, and clove are the core ingredients of a controlling powder. They are all fiery herbs that command attention and cause others to submit to your will. Rose, mixed with clover honey, lime, and bay, creates sexual power and summons others' desires to please you and serve your sexual needs. Prepare a bowl of powdered allspice, cinnamon, clove, crushed red rose petals, and bay leaves. Add drops of lime juice and a drizzle of clover honey. Stir and keep out in the bedroom. *This spell is only effective when used on an intimate partner. Do not attempt to use this on a stranger or someone you are not yet involved with.*

Work Control Spell

Ingredients:

> allspice
> cinnamon
> clove
> ginger
> lemon and orange peel

This is to be used when you need a job done and you want to force someone else to do it. It can also be used to be more commanding and will cause others to treat you more respectfully at work. Allspice, cinnamon, and clove are the central controlling ingredients. Ginger steps up the actions of those you want to command. Lemon and orange make others feel generous toward you.

Prepare a bowl of powdered allspice, cinnamon, clove, ginger, lemon and orange peel, and leave out in the workplace. Dust your hands with this mixture when you need to gain control. The blend should summon service with a smile.

SPELL TO WOO A CLIENT OR BOSS

Ingredients:

> yellow rose
> jar of honey

rum or imitation rum
green plantain

Open a jar of honey and pluck all the petals off a yellow rose. Drop the petals into the jar and let the petals sink into the honey. Slice a green plantain lengthwise, place on a plate, and pour all the honey into the crevice of the plantain. The honey will probably spill over into the plate. This is fine. Take a shot glass of rum or imitation rum flavoring and pour on top of the honey. Put this mixture outside or in front of an open window overnight. Leave it in place until it attracts flies or any type of insect. Once it has attracted bugs, dip your pointer fingers inside the plantain and anoint the pulse points of your wrists with your pointer fingers. Use the right finger to anoint the left wrist and the left finger to anoint the right wrist. Hold your fingers in this position for several minutes. Focus on your pulse until you can feel or hear it on both sides. Then visualize the client or boss being receptive to your proposal. This final meditation and closure of the spell must be completed when three stars appear in the evening sky. This can be the evening of or the evening before your meeting. After the meditation, you may dispose of the contents on the plate outside under a healthy tree or a compost.

Yellow roses symbolize success and are sacred to Oshun, the Yoruban goddess who teaches the art of wooing. She also rules gold. Honey is also sacred to Oshun, but we use it in this spell for its power of attraction. Rum is sacred to Ellegua and Chango. Ellegua opens channels and removes obstacles and Chango rules business acumen. The plantain is also sacred to Ellegua and Chango, and the green is used to attract money. Insects are believed to be the children of deities, and it is always a favorable sign that your offering is pleasing to the gods when insects are drawn. The pointer finger is ruled by Jupiter. Jupiter increases wealth and gives power in all business affairs. The wrist or any pulse point is a magical entry point to infuse yourself with any type of energy. If you visualize anything while connecting with a pulse point it adds life and probable manifestation to your visualization. According to lunar calendar laws, the evening begins when three stars appear in the sky. Also, three is the magic number of wish fulfillment.

To tap into someone's hidden desires, dip your pinkies into the plaintain and then press both pinkies against the third eye. The pinkies are ruled by Mercury, and the third eye (in the middle of your forehead) will add clairvoyance to your communication. A client of mine was entertaining a very important Japanese patron. She did this spell and the client was dazzled at how she entertained him. She gave him the New York he had always imagined. Needless to say, he invested all his company's money in her project.

THE BOSS'S WIFE SPELL

Ingredients:

> **sage**
> **lime**
> **rose**
> **lavender**
> **walnuts**

Have you ever made a bad impression by coming on too strong or having too much sexual appeal or just looking too damn good? This spell is designed for making the right impression. Whether you are meeting the boss's wife, a prospective client, or an inlaw, you want to come off looking and feeling your best. In certain situations it is inappropriate to emit a sexual or seductive vibration. In fact sometimes it can be completely deadly. There is a certain competitive spirit, especially between heterosexual women, that can create negative energy. If a woman feels sexually threatened by another woman the relationship begins on the wrong foot and very rarely gets rectified. The spell can also be used by women who need to make strong impressions on men without attracting the men on a sexual level. This spell will help you look and feel your best without being threatening. Beauty, grace, and strength can be revealed without the seductive edge.

Sage has been used by Native American cultures to cleanse the aura of any negativity. It is also used in modern magic to eliminate excessive sexual vibrations. Imaging in modern advertising teaches us that sexuality is equivalent to looking good. It suggests that a woman is only looking good if she looks "hot." Magically and psychologically women find other women less threatening when they can connect or relate to the other's masculine side or even neutral side. The sage is a neutralizer.

Lime is a fruit of power, control, and influence. By itself it can be a bit strong. However, combined with more feminine herbs, it adds a touch of masculinity to a woman that can be interpreted as strength. Rose and lavender are both feminine flowers of love yet they open love from the heart chakra (unconditional love) as opposed to the root chakra (sexual love). Rose is often combined with sexual herbs to add the element of altruism or friendship to a romance. When rose is combined with lavender it produces a state of grace.

Walnuts are a magical brain food. Adding walnuts to the above ingredients can make you more mentally (as opposed to physically) seductive. Usually the head is associated with yang, or male, attributes, whereas the body is associated with more yin, or feminine, attributes. Compare the patriarchal creation myths with those of the matriarchy. The male god conceived an idea in his *mind*, spoke the word, and the world was created (e.g., Athena being born out of the head of Zeus). In the matriarchal myths the world was born out of the *womb* of the goddess. Lime and walnut stimulate the creative centers of the brain. When a woman brings up her subtle yang energies it produces a nonthreatening attitude and therefore one of more openness to other women. In relation to the opposite sex, it creates grounds for equal opportunity and takes the awareness off of the genitalia.

This potion can be prepared in two ways. The first is a bath that should be taken in the early evening before your encounter. Draw a bath of warm water and add a quarter cup of crushed sage, the juice of two limes, a quarter cup each of dried rose and lavender flowers, and a teaspoon of crushed walnuts. Soak in the tub for ten minutes and then rinse off with water only. This method is best used for a single encounter.

If you anticipate several encounters throughout the week or month, prepare a ouanga bag to carry with you at all times. Fill a zipper-lock plastic bag with equal parts sage, rose, and lavender. Squeeze in the juice of one lime, and add the meat of three walnuts. You must then activate the ouanga by lighting a match, dropping it in the bag and quickly blowing it out. Spit in the bag and then seal the zipper lock. You should carry this ouanga bag in a purse or pocket and keep it concealed.

BOND GIRL SPELL

Ingredients:

mango
lime
rose water
venison
seven pea pods

cinnamon gum
lavender sachet or soap

When she walked into the room, every head turned. That's because only hours earlier she had eaten a mango and pulled the fruit's flesh from its pit. Then she had taken the pulpy pit and rubbed her entire body with it. Mango is the fruit of compelling beauty and it attracts suitors like bees to honey. After anointing with the mango, she mixed herself a lime spritzer while drawing a bath of rose water and venison.* Rose water is sacred to Venus, goddess of beauty and love. Venison is sacred to Diana, goddess of the hunt. The lime of course gave her power and influence over all she met. Hours later, way beyond the witching hour, when everyone else started to fade, her beauty took on an even greater depth. She glowed in the wee hours. That's because the night before she had placed seven pea pods under her pillow to make sure she got plenty of beauty sleep. Pea pods are also sacred to Venus. They have the added attribute of creating peace and tranquility and it is a known fact that a stress-free body retains its good looks.

She had a witty and intelligent comeback for every encounter as she circulated the room. That's because she chewed a piece of cinnamon gum on the way in. Cinnamon is sacred to Mercury. He grants the powers of persuasive speech, humor, charm, and eloquent conversation. She also put a lavender sachet in her shoe. Lavender brings peace and protection. It is also sacred to Mercury or Hermes, the patron god of thieves. It was with ease and grace that she surreptitiously slipped the microchip into her maidenform. The congressman never suspected a thing, and by the time he placed his hand into his inside breast pocket to check his goods, she was safe and sound and speeding toward Baghdad.

---

*You can find venison at the butcher shop. Place a small bone in your bath water.

Luck Be a Lady Tonight

PROSPERITY WATER SPELL

Ingredients:

ten pennies
empty jar
green food coloring
green candle
potting soil

This is a modern spell I have designed by combining several ancient customs. The results are quite effective. In order to begin the spell you must first obtain ten pennies, preferably ones found on a road or street. There is an old belief about picking up pennies that I will share with you. Only pick up a penny that is facing heads up. If you come across a penny that is tails up, do not pick it up for it will bring you bad luck. According to magical etiquette, you should flip that penny so that it faces heads up and leave it in place to bring another good luck!

Once you have your ten pennies, place them in an empty clear jar. Fill the jar with spring water and three drops of green food coloring. On the next full moon leave the jar (lid off) under the light of the moon. You may place it on a windowsill where the moon is sure to shine, or in a garden or terrace. If you do not have access to any of these places, go outside with the jar and hold it up to the light of the full moon for at least thirteen minutes. The longer the jar is exposed, the more powerful the potion, but thirteen minutes is the minimum amount of time required to empower the water. You must close the lid on the jar and take it inside before sunrise. On the following evening, seal the lid of the jar by dripping the wax of a green candle round and round the perimeter of the jar, sealing the space between the neck of the jar and the lid. Bury the jar in some rich dark earth. You can do this outside in a garden or indoors with a pot and some potting soil. Once you have buried the jar, trace an invoking pentagram (five-pointed star) on the surface of the soil. To draw an invoking pentagram begin at the top point and move down diagonally to the left. Continue up diagonally to the center right point. Go across horizontally to the center left point. Move down diagonally to the bottom right point and continue up diagonally to meet the original top center point. If you visualize the pentagram as a person standing with arms and legs outstretched this should be easy to imagine. The top center point is the head. The right and left center points are the arms and the right and left bottom points of the star are the legs.

So, *the head bone connected to the left leg. Left leg connected to the right arm. Right arm connected to the left arm. Left arm connected to the right leg. Right leg connected to the head bone. Now you've done the pentagram all on your own.*

The pentagram is a symbol of earth and prosperity. By burying your jar in the earth you are infusing it with the power of the earth goddess. The copper of the pennies also represents the earth element. Pentagram, soil, and copper infuse your water with the triple aspect of earth, therefore the water will be thrice blessed. Keep the jar buried until the next new moon. Wait 24 additional hours and then dig up the jar. Break the wax seal and sprinkle this water around home, business, or person anytime you want to bring more prosperity into your life.

HOW TO BREAK A LOSING STREAK

Ingredients:

> **steel wool**
> **sage**
> **bay**
> **black cat kitchen magnet**
> **molasses**
> **three hairs from a black cat**

Seymour was a loser with a heart of gold. Seymour was constantly throwing parties to which no one would come. It would take him six months to work up enough courage to ask a woman out. Then when he finally got up the nerve, on the night of his date, he would come down with the flu and his Jeep would break down. The first time Seymour had a bit of extra cash in the bank, he decided to try his luck on the stock exchange. That was the same day the market fell over 500 points. Seymour needed some serious help.

Witches believe that if a black cat crosses your path, you will have incredible *good* luck. There is actually an old formula from a book of shadows called Black Cat Powder.* It is used to turn around a losing streak. I have adapted the

*Herman Slater, ed., *The Magickal Formulary* (New York: Magickal Childe Pub. Inc., 1981).

spell using modern substitutes for some of the more difficult-to-obtain ancient ingredients. Myrrh, although easily obtainable in occult supply shops, cannot be found in the supermarket. Molasses, also ruled by Saturn, contains similar properties to myrrh and can be used as a substitute. Iron or lodestones were used because of their magnetic properties. A kitchen magnet contains the same attracting properties as a lodestone. If you can find a kitchen magnet in the shape of a black cat, the spell will become even more effective. If you are not able to obtain one, detach the magnetic back off of any design. It is also possible to buy plain magnetic strips.

There is no substitute for three black cat hairs. If you do not own a black cat, try a neighbor or local pet store. You can also try checking out the back alley of your local supermarket or deli. There may be a black cat lurking there. Most important rule of thumb in obtaining three black cat hairs: *you must not harm or frighten the animal in any way.* This would be extremely bad luck and destroy the potency of the spell. An easy way to obtain the hairs is to pull them from a cat brush. You can also befriend the animal and give it a good rub. Usually a few stray hairs will come loose. Let the cat sit in your lap and you will probably find more than three cat hairs stuck to your clothing.

The rest of the ingredients remain true to the original recipe. Take a piece of steel wool and stretch it out so that it becomes more porous. Sprinkle a tablespoon each of crushed sage and crushed bay leaves into the steel wool. Drop the magnet onto the steel wool and drizzle molasses over it. Let the three black cat hairs float down and stick to the molasses. Fold up the steel wool and place in a zipper-lock baggie or fold up in a square of tinfoil. Carry with you to increase your good fortune.

Seymour took this little package to Las Vegas and made quite a pretty penny.

He traded in the Jeep for a more reliable chauffeur and limo. He also met a beautiful showgirl and has invited her to go scuba diving in the Bahamas (the least likely place to catch a winter cold).

LUCKY PIG SPELL

Ingredients:

nutmeg, whole
lard

Crossculturally, many ancient religions used the pig, or wild boar, as a totem of their godhead. Because of its sacredness, taboos arose against eating pig. Later on, in an attempt to crush the memory of these ancient gods, the pig became known as unclean and unlucky, and taboos against eating them were fortified.

The poor pig finally said "hogwash" and somehow turned his image around. For many centuries, the pig has now been associated with luck and prosperity. For people living in farmlands, pigs represented wealth. They were used as legal tender and could feed whole families through a cold winter.

In Germany you will find popular talismans of tiny pigs molded out of copper with pfennigs* glued to their backs. The piggy bank is a relatively modern image. It was created by accident around the eighteenth century. The high costs of mined metal caused people to use an inexpensive orange clay called pygg to make jars and other household items. The pygg bank was eventually molded in the shape of a pig.

*pennies

There is nothing luckier than lard or the fat of a pig. Rub a dab of lard around a whole nutmeg** and use it for a gambler's luck talisman.

ROOT ROOT ROOT FOR THE HOME TEAM SPELL

Ingredients:

> **candles in assorted colors**
> **cinnamon powder**
> **bay leaves**
> **spearmint**
> *and/or*
> **red sage**
> **chili powder**
> **black pepper**
> **cinnamon**
> **pinch of sulfur**

In the mid-80s, a fellow witch and I decided our favorite National League baseball team needed a little help in winning the World Series. They had disappointed us beyond reason and there was nothing else to resort to but some miracle magic to push them over the top. We obtained two candles representing our team colors (in this case orange and blue*) and rubbed them vigorously with cinnamon powder,

---

**Nutmeg increases the intuition.
*Orange also happens to be the color of Mercury, that swift and clever god of success. Blue is a color representing the benevolence of Jupiter.

spearmint, and crushed bay leaves. Cinnamon is used to win the favor of the gods. Bay laurel was traditionally used to crown the victors in the ancient Greek Olympics. Spearmint attracts kindly spirits (and sometimes crafty elementals). I lit the candles and visualized our team winning.

My associate, who is a bit more unscrupulous than I, decided that we needed to do something to weaken the other team as well. We were all out of the candle colors representing the opposing team. However, my associate had been wearing a pair of crimson socks, which he felt would adequately represent the opposition. He removed a sock from his foot and pulled it over his hand like a glove. He held out his palm and sprinkled it with red sage, chili powder, black pepper, cinnamon, and a pinch of sulfur (which he scraped off a match head). These ingredients form a very famous crossing agent known as Hot Foot powder. It is used to shake the confidence of your opponents and trip them up. My partner then carefully pulled the sock off his hand, turning it inside out, and tied it in a knot. By this time, it was the bottom of the tenth and things didn't look too promising. The score was tied. We had two outs, two strikes, four singles in a row, and were one strike away from losing. The candles burned dimly on top of the console and looked as if they were about to go out. My partner squatted in front of the television set and quietly pounded his magic pouch into his fist. At this point, we had a man on second and a man at bat. The batter hit a ground ball down to first base. The ball went under the first baseman's glove and into the outfield. Our man on second made it home and scored the winning run. The morning papers described the victory as a major miracle. One report claimed that the triumph was tainted with mischievous magic. My associate calmly folded up the sports section after reading that line, cocked his head slyly and said, ''It gets by Buckner!''

GOOD SMOKE SPELL

Ingredients:

cigar, the more expensive, the better

Enjoying a good smoke after dinner is more than just relaxing, it is magical. In Native American tradition, smoke is used to carry prayers or messages. In Latin American tradition, smoke is used to feed and petition the Orishas (gods). Cigar smoke is sacred to both Ellegua and Chango. Ellegua is the remover of obstacles and problems. Chango is the ruler of business success and good character. Next time you take an important client out to dinner be sure to smoke a good cigar after supper to remove all obstacles from your path and to bring success and integrity to your business endeavor. To please these two Orishas even further, order shots of rum for all at the table. Order two extra shots for Ellegua and Chango. Leave these glasses untouched but blow cigar smoke over the glasses. This should be done by ''shotgunning'': Carefully place the lit end of the cigar in your mouth and blow smoke out the other end into the rum glasses. Give three smoke signals for Ellegua and six for Chango.

MISSION IMPOSSIBLE SPELL

Part I

Annie needed a miracle. Her husband (and his income) had left her. Her mother had become very ill and Annie needed days free to take her mother to various doctor appointments. No longer able to work the nine to five, she needed a job with flexible evening hours, not to mention good pay, and excellent benefits. The job also had to be in the arts. Annie lived in a special rent-controlled building. One of the requirements for living there was that a certain percentage of your income had to be earned in the entertainment field.

"Listen," said Annie, "I've been eating potatoes and onions for the past few weeks. I've really had to tighten my belt. Could you get me something within walking distance? I don't have money for bus fare and I don't have any money to spend on a new wardrobe. I need some kind of job where I can just show up in jeans."

"Well, Annie," I said, "that's quite a tall order."

Annie was also fed up with show-biz creeps. I guess that's why she hadn't even looked in the trade papers for any jobs.

"One more request: If I have to work around men, let them be gorgeous hunks with poetry flowing from their mouths, or fags with impeccable taste. And I'd like to work around more well-rounded women, European, perhaps, or . . ."

"Annie, Annie, give me a break," I said. "You want more culture in your life. I got it! We'll see what we can do."

One thing I admired about Annie; she was very clear about her needs. Magical intent is one of the most important ingredients in a spell. Never back away from what you truly require. The gods are always drawn to ardent desire.

I went home and pulled out the Mission Impossible file from my Grimoire and emptied all of its contents onto my altar. I created a large bowl of potpourri using a sprinkle of **lime** peels and dried **wintergreen** leaves, to compel and attract friendly and powerful spirits to assist us. Wintergreen is very Mercurial and I thought it might help with those flexible hours Annie requested. To surround Annie with powerful artistic types, I added fresh white, yellow, and red **carnation** petals, **gardenia** soap shavings, and jasmine rice.

An old witch friend of mine, who is a clotheshorse and incredible fashion designer, swears by a talisman she created by rubbing cotton with jasmine. She says it always inspires her clothing designs. I pulled apart a piece of **cotton** and rubbed it vigorously between my palms along with a handful of uncooked **jasmine** rice. I let the bits of cotton and rice fall into the bowl after they had been heated by my hands. I hoped this might solve Annie's wardrobe dilemma. One hundred and twenty whole **cloves**, seven crushed **bay** leaves, and a pinch of loose **Earl Grey tea** (which contains bergamot oil) were added to open doors and channels for success. A wet **apple** peel and one capful each of **cherry** and **vanilla** extracts were mixed in to bring about bounty and incredible good fortune. The combination of florals and fruits is also alleged to bring pleasing news or sounds to the ear. Bay, bergamot, and carnation combined improve the health. Annie's mom needed healing and Annie needed to stay healthy to care for her. I was concerned after hearing about her horrible eating habits. I added a teaspoon of **goat's milk** to richen Annie's diet.

Now for the real miracle. There is a magical term called "sphere of availability." The narrower the sphere, the slimmer your chances for manifestation. For example, if you want to win the lotto, you must play. The more lotto tickets you buy, the more you increase your chances (sphere of availability) of winning. A spell is like a baited fishing line. Increasing the sphere of availability creates a pond full of hungry fish. Annie wasn't doing much to increase the odds. She wasn't exactly pounding the pavement and I wondered where this job was going to materialize from. Since Annie was a lapsed Catholic, I added a teaspoon of **olive oil** and a lovely white and yellow **rose** petal. Olive and rose are sacred to St. Jude, patron saint of the impossible.

Bay and olive are also sacred to Apollo, god of the arts. In Greece they were worn as symbols of triumph and achievement. It seemed all my mixing and matching would work. I could think of no ill side effects by combining all these numerous ingredients. Well, hmm, there was that medieval black magic spell where limes were pricked with cloves. It was performed to bring great tragedy into someone's life. I gazed warily into my magic potion bowl and absentmindedly separated some clove thorns that had lodged themselves into lime peels. "Damn it, she'll just have to take her chances," I thought. The hour was late and I was not about to prepare another mixture.

"May the gods and St. Jude be with you, Annie," I chanted while giving the potion a final stir.

The next morning, I took a large **orange candle*** and carved Annie's name and astrological sign into it. I rolled the candle in the bowl and generously covered it

---

* *A note concerning these ingredients:* Many supermarkets sell fresh flowers, and it is best to obtain fresh carnations, roses, gardenias, and jasmine flowers. If you cannot find these fresh flowers, they are also very popular scents found in air fresheners or soaps. Simply spray the air freshener into your mixture or add shavings of scented soaps. For jasmine flowers you may substitute jasmine rice. Extracts, dried herbs, or fruit juices are also interchangeable (in the case of cherry, apple, and vanilla). Use whatever you can get your hands on.

with the mixture. I delivered the candle to Annie and instructed her to light it and pray over it. About a month later, on the next new moon, I received a call from this witch friend of mine, you know, the costume designer. She was moving on to bigger and better things, and she wanted to know if I, or anyone I knew, was interested in this job.

"What kind of job?" I asked. "A what—a dresser! At the where? The Metropolitan Opera? Really? More culture than you can shake a broomstick at!" I passed Annie's phone number along.

Annie jumped at the job. She began dressing the principals, and occasionally she was called to work a matinee. Still, the job gave her plenty of quality time with mom and fulfilled the legal requirements she needed to keep her apartment. Although she zips divas into some of the most beautiful gowns in the world, Annie can come to work in any old *schmatah*. Dressers dress down and need their clothes to be functional for stocking safety pins in case Aida pops a seam. The job is also in walking distance and I understand Annie is eating better.

"Placido throws huge parties for the whole company. It's a rare night you walk by and not see something on the table in the principals' area," Annie told me.

Last year Annie switched to dressing the ballet, because the hours are even more flexible. Operas voted the most fun are *Boris Godunov* and *Peter Grimes*.

"It's just a matter of changing a few shawls throughout the evening," laughs Annie.

While tragedy and ruin unfold center stage, it's "any excuse for a party" in the wings. There was one real tragedy that did unfold; a patron threw himself off the balcony in the middle of the "Scottish play," but luckily, Annie was off that performance. In the words of one of the great Wagnerian mezzo sopranos, Annie's life has gone "from *schlimm* to *schlemm*"!

Part II

After setting Annie up, I decided to give this spell a whirl myself. My request was simply this: great opera seats. Of course Annie provides me with free standing room tickets whenever I ask, but each time I perform this ritual, someone with season tickets mysteriously does not attend that evening's performance. With stealth and attitude, I glide into the box or empty orchestra seat the gods have assigned me.

The following spells are to be done on specific nights of the week. Each night has certain ruling energies or influences. Use this guide to enhance each night of the week, and change your life year-round.

MONDAY EVENINGS

Monday, or *Moon*day, is a night considered sacred to all lunar goddesses. All water signs (Cancer, Scorpio, Pisces) do well performing magic on a Monday night. Monday is a night for any sort of emotional magic, love, healing, protection, and strengthening psychic powers. If the moon is waxing (new to full) on a Monday night, it is good to petition the moon goddess for increase. During a waning (full to new) moon, obstacles and negative situations can be removed. What follows is an assortment of simple spells for Monday night moon magic. All ingredients used in these spells are considered to be under lunar rule.

FOR PROTECTION

Ingredients:

blueberries

Eat blueberries or blueberry yogurt on a waxing moon to add protection to your aura. On a waning moon, smash blueberries in a bowl and yell out your fears as you do so. This is an excellent banishing ritual. After the blueberries have been smashed, wash them down the drain with water and visualize your fears being washed away as well.

FOR LOVE

Ingredients:

eggs
mushrooms
red bell peppers
hot chocolate or cocoa
lemon
papaya

On a waxing moon prepare a mushroom omelet with red bell peppers to increase the glamour and sex in your relationship. If you are single, drink hot chocolate to add the power of attraction to your spell.

To remove obstacles in the love life, take a bath with one whole raw unbroken egg and the juice of one whole fresh lemon. Do this on a waning moon Monday. Stay in the tub for at least ten minutes. Then let the water drain and dispose of the egg outside your home. After the bath, drink a cup of hot water with lemon and ten drops of papaya juice. Lemon and egg remove negative emotional energy. Papaya is a sex food and also renews energy and hope.

FOR PSYCHIC AWARENESS

Ingredients:

dish towel
poppy seeds
small jar

This spell can be performed on a Monday night regardless of the phase of the moon. New and waxing moons generally renew or add to the development of your psychic powers. Full moons strengthen existing power and waning or dark moons unlock hidden potential. Spread a clean dish towel or paper towel on a table or counter. Draw an eye by sprinkling poppy seeds onto the towel. Bow your head over the towel and press your third eye (located in the center of your forehead) against the poppy seed eye. Remain in this position for three minutes. Lift your head and stare at the poppy seeds. Lick your fingers and press them into the poppy. Some seeds should stick to your fingers. Ingest the poppy seeds that are on your fingers. Pour the remaining seeds into a small jar and shake the jar around your head. Around midnight you can begin whatever psychic work you have planned. Continue to shake the jar around your head to enhance your psychic energy.

WAXING MOON SPELL FOR PROSPERITY

Ingredients:

lettuce
pumpkin
seaweed
green grapes

Lettuce, pumpkin, seaweed, and green grapes are all foods associated with prosperity. They are also foods ruled by the moon. Eat all or add some to your regular diet every Monday night from the new to full moon period to magically manifest prosperity into your life.

WANING MOON SPELL TO WARD OFF POVERTY

Ingredients:

cabbage
lemon
salt
mayonnaise
lentil soup

Perform this spell every Monday night from the full to dark moon period to eliminate financial worries. Shred some cabbage and mix in a bowl with a dollop

of mayonnaise, the juice from a lemon, and a dash of salt. You can also u͟
bought cole slaw, but it is more effective to prepare the salad yourself. Ca͟
is a prosperity food used to protect income or uncover hidden income. Lemon a͟
salt are purifiers. Mayonnaise also contains lemon and salt, as well as vinegar and
eggs, which remove negativity and obstacles. Sugar, used to sweeten life, is also
found in mayonnaise, and a final ingredient, soybeans, bring good fortune.

You can also eat lentil soup. Lentils are considered a staple food and are eaten
to deliver people through hard times.

FOR A PEACEFUL HOME

Ingredients:

> **cucumbers**
> **salt**
> **lemon juice**
> **white wine**

Cucumbers are sacred to the moon and add peaceful vibrations to home and
family. You can add cucumbers to your regular diet or eat them alone, salted, any
Monday night. Also try eating cucumbers with a dash of salt and a spritz of lemon
juice on a Monday night to keep you stress-free for the week ahead. Cucumbers
marinated in white wine can be ingested to relieve tension between married couples.
Wine is used in sacred rites of many traditions. White wine invokes the lunar
goddess in her wise aspect, and when combined with cucumber it bestows the
couple with calmness and intuitive wisdom to deal with one another compassion-
ately.

TUESDAY EVENINGS

Tuesday is ruled by the planet and the god Mars. If we look at the name of the day in Spanish, *martes*, its origin is clearer. Tuesday-night magic should revolve around health, stamina, sexuality, and success at winning battles. The following are some ritual suggestions. All potions include food and products sacred to the fiery Mars.

SPELL FOR SEXUAL STAMINA

Ingredients:

chocolate-covered bananas
basil
carrots

Chocolate and banana would be considered a quick-fix spell. They can be combined and eaten in a pinch to immediately increase the sexual appetite. Basil and carrots can be added to salads on a regular basis to maintain your sexual stamina.

SPELL FOR VICTORY

Ingredients:

watercress
mustard
leeks
coffee
spinach

Watercress was eaten by the Romans in order to outwit their enemies. Mustard, leeks, and coffee increase physical stamina. Spinach, sacred to both Mars and Jupiter, is also the favorite of that modern-day Hercules, Popeye the Sailorman. (Never underestimate the power of a modern-day myth!)

On a Tuesday night, before your next battle, steam some leeks, spinach, and watercress. Season with hot mustard seed and eat. Follow up with a cup of black coffee or bathe in a tub of warm water with a freshly brewed pot of coffee added to the bath water.

SPELL FOR HEALTH AND ENERGY

Ingredients:

spinach
garlic

ginger
cayenne pepper

Each part of the body is ruled by a planet and/or astrological sign. Mars is the ruler of the head. Although not all illnesses are mind over matter, and *these spells are not substitutes for seeking medical advice,* witches do believe that positive thinking promotes positive energies in the physical body. Eating garlic or ginger is a magical preventative against catching a head cold. Drinking hot water with a pinch of cayenne pepper mixed in can clear the sinuses, wake up all the senses, and is believed to flush the body of toxins. For an invigorating psychic and mental cleanser, rub the top of the head with fresh ginger root. This will help to awaken the brain and as a result give you more physical energy. Whole ginger root has also been used in poppet magic. You must use a root with two legs. Ginger roots actually look more like teeth than human bodies. Carve your name or the name of the person you are trying to heal into the body of the ginger root. On a Tuesday morning, place it on a windowsill in the sun. On Sunday at sunset, remove the root, and you, or the person you are trying to heal, may carry the root as a talisman. Simply place in the pocket or tie a string around the ginger root and wear it around the neck.

Mars is generally invoked to heal blood problems, muscle aches, head injuries, or internal bleeding, and to create more physical stamina in the body. Rub affected areas of the external body with raw spinach leaves to invoke the vibrant healing energy of Mars. For other health issues, check spells in the **Sunday Evenings** section.

SPELL FOR SUCCESS

Ingredients:

basil
pine nuts

Mars success spells are most useful when beating out competition is necessary for you to win. Mars spells are also effective to use if you want to win at sports events. Basil is also known as the "witches herb." It is a powerful plant with many uses. Generally it is known to rule the drive and ambition of a person. If mixed with love herbs, basil enhances the sex drive. Combined with herbs for success, it will enhance the competitive drive or will to succeed. Pine nuts were popular in Rome and eaten to create more physical strength. The combination of basil and pine will strengthen your will and your physical body and thereby increase your chances of competing and winning. Wrap five pine nuts in a basil leaf and eat on a Tuesday night or make a tinfoil pouch with five pine nuts and five basil leaves to carry with you as a magical talisman for success. You can also prepare a pesto sauce and serve to your teammates before a big competition.

SPELL TO TURN THE ENERGY OF YOUR ENEMIES AGAINST THEMSELVES

Ingredients:

   shoelace (red or black)
   ginger
   black pepper
   small mirror

Mars is a fighter and a protector. The god and planet rules quarreling and confusion. If you feel someone is working against you, magically or physically, do
this spell on a Tuesday night. Take a red or black (colors of Mars) shoelace and
tie it in a knot. As you do this, visualize the energy of your enemy looping around
and turning back to singe the sender. Now set fire to a corner of the knot in the
shoelace. Rub the fire out in a plate of powdered ginger. Sprinkle black pepper on
top of the shoelace once it has been extinguished. Take the shoelace and rub it
counterclockwise around the reflective side of a small mirror. Place this mirror in
a window of your house with the reflective side facing out. This will keep any
harm or ill will from affecting you.

Shoelaces are used because they are connected with the shoes, which lead us in
life. A shoelace can trip someone up. Knotting is a witch's form of magic to bind
or turn something around. We burn the knot to attract the attention of Mars, as he
loves fire. Ginger and pepper are herbs that instigate and can be used to cause
trouble or confusion. Mirrors rubbed with these herbs can be used as boomerangs
to send back negative energy.

WEDNESDAY EVENINGS

"Wednesday's child is full of woe." The old adage would have us believe that children born on a Wednesday are sad folk. Not so. *Wo* actually refers to Woden/Odin, the Teutonic/Norse god this day of the week takes its name from. In German the day was called Wodens Tag (Woden's Day) and then changed to Mittwoch (Midweek) in an attempt by the Church to banish the memory of the old pagan god. Woden's temples were destroyed by Augustine, but the ruins of his shrines can be seen at the abbey of Canterbury in Great Britain. Woden is the god of wisdom, learning, and the wind. Sailors would pray to him for a strong breeze to catch up their sails, so it would be more accurate to say those born on this day are full of *gusto*. Woden was incorporated into the Roman god Mercury and we see his name in the Spanish *miércoles* and the French *mercredi*. Mercury was the messenger of the gods. He rules communication, writing, speech, poetry, and creative endeavors. The following are spells using Mercurial ingredients and are all to be performed on a Wednesday night.

SPELL FOR SUCCESS

Ingredients:

orange candles
almond oil
dried beans

_ange is the color of success. Almonds are used for love, money, and success. ıs believed that climbing an almond tree will bring success in business. I suggest anointing orange candles with almond oil. Start at the bottom of the candle and work your way up, as if you were climbing a tree. Once the candle is lit, carefully place a drop of wax on eight dried beans. Eight is the number of Mercury, and beans, ruled by Mercury, bring good luck. After the wax dries, carry the beans in your pocket. The beans can also be shaken in the right fist before or during a situation in which you need success.

SPELL FOR INSPIRATION AND CREATIVITY

Ingredients:

> **cinnamon**
> **pine oil**
> **clove**
> **wintergreen**
> **lavender or rose**

This blend is said to open the mind and summon the muse. Clove, pine, and cinnamon clear the head of mundane thoughts and are said to strengthen the creative muscles. Wintergreen and rose or lavender were used by bards and poets to keep their muses at hand. Mix cinnamon powder, eight drops of pine oil, a handful of cloves, three drops of spirit of wintergreen,* and a half cup of lavender or rose petals into a bowl. Stir eight times clockwise and place the bowl on your altar or

*Spirit of wintergreen can usually be found in a pharmacy.

place where you do your creative work. Let it stand as a potpourri and ʌ̣
to your face and inhale deeply or run your fingers through the blend wheɪɪ
need inspiration.

SPELL FOR LEARNING AND KNOWLEDGE

Ingredients:

caraway
spearmint
walnut
hazelnut

Caraway and spearmint are alleged to jog the memory. They should be chewed while studying or memorizing information. Walnuts stimulate the conscious mind and are said to stimulate thinking. It is not enough to memorize information; the brain must also process the information and utilize it. Hazelnut is the nut of wisdom. It can be eaten to gain true understanding of a subject. Keep all four ingredients handy to chew and munch on to increase your learning abilities.

SPELL FOR COMMUNICATION

Ingredients:

fennel (water)
dill (air)
marjoram (earth)

ft the bowl
ver you

al herbs of communication. Fennel opens the emotional cen-
. Dill is very airy and opens the intellect. It can also be used
it. Marjoram rules the earth plane and helps with practical
...unication. Cinnamon is fiery and promotes not just talking but taking action.
Nutmeg rules the spirit or psychic plane and adds the intuitive element to your communication. Use all five herbs to promote well rounded rapport. Place small bits under the tongue for a few moments or mix a potpourri with generous amounts of each.

THURSDAY EVENINGS

Thursday takes its name from the god of thunder, Thor. Another god who ruled
the lighting rod was Jupiter or Jove. *Jueves* is the Spanish word for Thursday and
it is derived from Jove. Jupiter is the god of expansions. He brings material as
well as spiritual gain. He is also known to grant an all-seeing eye of protection.
The following are spells to be performed on a Thursday night. All ingredients are
sacred to and approved by Jove.

SPELL FOR FINANCIAL GAIN

Ingredients:

millet

Millet is believed to bring prosperity in both Chinese and European lore. You can add millet to your diet on Thursdays or just run the fine uncooked grain through your hands while visualizing your income increasing. Millet can also be sprinkled in the corners of a home or business to draw money.

SPELL FOR PROTECTION

Ingredients:

sage
cedar

Sage and cedar are burned by Native Americans for cleansing and protection. Both herbs are ruled by Jupiter and should be burned to best utilize their energy. If the sage leaves and cedar chips are dry enough they should ignite. Place in a pot of cast iron or stone and walk around the entire house clockwise with the smoldering cauldron.

The second-best method is to boil water and make an infusion. Soak the herbs in a quart of boiled water for twenty minutes. Strain the herbs and then add to mop water and wash down the whole house. If you have carpeting, let tea cool, fill a spray bottle, and mist the air in every room.

SPELL FOR SPIRITUAL INSIGHT

Ingredients:

barley
star anise
purple candles

Star anise is used to increase intuition. If you find a whole root in the shape of a perfect star, you can carry it to clarify your purpose and direction in life. Barley is sacred to Jupiter, but also to his sister Demeter. It was Zeus who finally intervened on Demeter's behalf and forced Hades to release Persephone from the underworld. If you have a serious problem in life, barley will attract the benevolence of Jupiter to your aid. Purple is the color of wisdom and power.

Briefly describe your situation and inscribe some key descriptive words into a purple candle. Surround the candle with a circle of uncooked barley. Place a perfect star anise inside the circle of barley. When the candle has completed burning, place the star anise under your pillow to gain insight in your dreams. You can also carry the star anise with you to lead you in the right direction.

SPELL FOR INVESTMENTS AND BUSINESS EXPANSION

Ingredients:

fenugreek
spinach

dark green leafy lettuce
sprouts
nutmeg or star anise

The darker the lettuce, the deeper and stronger the prosperity it is alleged to draw. Fenugreek is eaten to expand wealth, and fenugreek seeds are sprinkled around a place of business to attract wealth. Spinach is a dark leafy green eaten to attract money and strength. Sprouts, because of their long branches, are believed to assist in financial expansions. Make a salad with all of these ingredients to promote business expansions. For investments add a pinch of powdered nutmeg or star anise over the salad to make you lucky and intuitive.

SPELL TO DISCOVER WHERE YOUR BEST INTERESTS LIE

Ingredients:

dark purple eggplant

Green, blue, and purple are all colors associated with Jupiter. Purple is the color representing power and insight. Eggplant is considered a food of wisdom and power. When used in association with the goddess Oya, it is associated with death and endings; however, when used in Jupiterian rituals it represents the joining of spiritual and material strengths.

In four words or less carve a situation that you need guidance with into an eggplant. Cook the eggplant and eat at least a quarter of it. You may dispose of the uneaten portion. You should begin to attract the people and situations that are most beneficial to you into your life. Repeat spell every Thursday until you notice significant change.

FRIDAY EVENINGS

Friday is sacred to Freya, the Norse equivalent of Venus. Notice the names of Friday in Spanish, *viernes,* and in Italian, *venerdi.* Venus is the goddess of friendship, courtship, romance, love, marriage, and family. The planet Venus is also associated with creativity and peace. The following are some Friday night spells all using Venusian ingredients.

FRIENDSHIP SPELL

Ingredients:

> **rose water or rose petals**
> **tangerines**

Rose, by itself, is the flower of friendship or courtship. If combined with certain ingredients it becomes a sexual blend. Tangerines, like oranges, are a fruit of love and commitment. Tangerines are more playful and do not suggest romantic commitment. This spell can be used to ward off unwanted sexual advances. I am not talking about situations that involve sexual harassment. (For spells of this nature check out *The Supermarket Sorceress* and *The Supermarket Sorceress's Sexy Hexes.*) I am talking about someone whom you genuinely care about, would like to become friends with, but unfortunately the poor fellow or gal is smitten with you. Before meeting up with the lovesick pup, bathe in a tub filled with the juice and pulp of three tangerines and a cup of rose water or white rose petals. This should help turn the nature of the relationship toward friendship.

To attract more friends into your life, eat tangerines and anoint the pulse points with rose water. You can also make a talisman of dried tangerine peel and white rose petals. Carry it in your pocket or purse when going out. You can also create a friendship altar by laying down a yellow cloth. Sprinkle white rose petals and dried tangerine peel over the cloth and add requests on small scraps of yellow paper describing the type of friends you would like to attract.

LOVE ATTRACTION SPELL

Ingredients:

> **lemon**
> **rose water**
> **vanilla bean or extract**
> **gold glitter or two gold stars**
> **almond oil**

This recipe comes from a New Orleans voodoo spell. Prepare a perfumed oil using almond oil as a base. Add seven drops of rose water, three drops of lemon extract or three drops of fresh lemon juice, a vanilla bean or seven drops of vanilla extract, and gold glitter or two gold stars. Anoint your pulse points before going out or add to bath water for a magical love attraction bath.

MARRIAGE SPELL

Ingredients:

> **tomato**
> **cardamom**
> **jasmine rice**

These three foods combined summon passion and commitment. Cook jasmine rice and add stewed tomatoes spiced with cardamom seeds. Eat to attract a marriage proposal. To influence someone to marry you, sprinkle uncooked jasmine rice, crushed sundried tomatoes, and crushed cardamom in a path he or she is sure to walk across.

HAPPY HOMEMAKER SPELL

Ingredients:

> **orange juice or orange slices**
> **peach juice or peach slices**
> **melon juice or melon balls**
> **lime**

In my first book, *The Supermarket Sorceress*, there are two spells entitled The Happy Homebreaker. The spells are utilized to catch a married man. There are also two spells to Ward Off the Happy Homebreaker. Interestingly (and surprisingly) enough, I have received numerous calls and letters from women concerning the first set of spells. They are checking and rechecking with me to make sure they are doing everything properly, and from most reports there seems to be a great level of success with their activity. Interestingly (and surprisingly), I have received no phone calls or letters from wives concerning the second set of spells. The following is just my way of evening the score as I offer yet another magical weapon of love to those defenseless and apparently inattentive first ladies.

Originally called Lucky Powder,* this blend is part of a well known collection of witches' brews. The formula is to prevent cheating in marriages, but the spell needs to be used before a deep emotional bond is formed between the offending parties. In other words, it will cut the grease of lust, but it won't remove the stain of love.

All ingredients are appealing to Aphrodite, and the spell should be performed on a Friday night. In Hebrew lore, Friday night is sacred to the Sabbath Queen or the Bride of God. It is traditionally a night set aside to honor the mothers and wives of the household. Prepare a drink of orange, peach, and melon juice with a lime wedge rubbed around the rim of the glass. Serve to your husband or partner with whom you wish to maintain a monogamous relationship. You may also serve a fruit salad with fresh orange, peach, and melon slices. Squeeze some lime juice and pulp over the fruit and serve for dessert. Tell your partner it's not only good for the figure but drives away the impulse to eat other sweets.

*Herman Slater, ed., *The Magickal Formulary* (New York: Magickal Childe Pub. Inc., 1981).

FAMILY HARMONY SPELL

Ingredients:

> **carob chips**
> **orange blossom honey**

Dip carob chips in orange blossom honey and serve to quarreling family members. You can also bake cookies using carob chips instead of chocolate and honey instead of sugar. Carob, unlike chocolate, does not carry any sexual vibrations. It is simply a food of love. Orange blossom honey reinforces that love and helps it stick through hard times. If the fight occurs between lovers or married couples, it is still wise to eat carob, for this way the matter will be resolved through the heart instead of the groin. Once this ritual has been performed you may bathe in vanilla extract (or bean) and rose water (or rose petals) to induce sexual healing.

SERENITY SPELL

Ingredients:

> **lavender**
> **sage**
> **lemon peel**
> **cardamom**

Lemon and sage tone down the sexual qualities of cardamom and the three combined bring serenity. Lavender added to the blend relaxes and eases any tension

that may be stored in the body. Take a bath in all these spice
them and keep it out in the family room to promote relaxation,

SATURDAY EVENINGS

Saturday is named after Saturn. In his heyday, Saturn was a big party god who liked drinking and merriment. The Roman celebration of Saturnalia was a big feast sending off the god for his time in the underworld. It was the last hurrah, so to speak, before the dark winter. No wonder Saturday night is traditionally the big night on the town.

Saturn or Cronos was eventually castrated by his son Zeus (Jupiter). After his death, he became associated with restrictions, power, death, ending, time, and lessons or karma in life. Saturn is also associated with Binah on the Quabalistic tree of life. Binah represents wisdom and sorrow. So there is an up and a down side to Saturn. The most positive elements are wisdom, power, purpose, and partying. On the down side, Saturn can leave you with one hell of a hangover.

SATURDAY NIGHT PARTY SPELL

Ingredients:

goat's milk
two or more cast-iron pots

Goats are the symbol of Capricorn, which is ruled by Saturn. According to Greek legend, goats were the nursemaids of the gods. The cornucopia, or horn of plenty, was created by Zeus from the horn of a goat. Drink goat's milk if you want to go ng like a god and be treated to the richness and plenty of life.

 iron, as well as all heavy metal, is also sacred to Saturn. If you are throwing a
 y at home, do this ritual to remove any restrictions from the night (unwanted
crashers, wet blanket neighbors who call the police, etc.). Walk counterclockwise
around your house and bang two or more cast-iron pots together. When you have
come full circle, turn around and bang clockwise to summon party power. If you are
going out, bang the pots in front of your body. Begin close to the body and move the
arms outward away from the body to remove restrictions (such as curfews, muggers,
bouncers, etc.). Then begin a second round of banging. This time start with your
hands out and move them closer to the body as you bang the pots. Shout out all the
fun elements you would like the evening to consist of. Happy Saturnalia!

SPELL TO MANIPULATE TIME

Ingredients:

a watch
a white candle

Of course you cannot really turn back time, unless you have a time machine.
This spell can be used for several reasons. The first is to recapture a moment or
feeling that you experienced sometime in the past. The second is to correct a
mistake or to heal an argument or misunderstanding that has ruined an evening.
Performing this spell can help you move beyond the anger or difficulty and get
back to where you started. The third use is to slow down time so that you can
fully enjoy every moment of the evening that you have planned.

For the first situation, take a watch and turn the hour hand back three full turns.

Close your eyes and allow your mind to take you back to the point in time that you wish to return to. Open your eyes and make another three full turns counterclockwise with the hour hand, moving faster this time. Close your eyes again and visualize the scene to which you wish to return. Open your eyes and make another three full turns back. This time begin turning fast and slow it down gradually. At the end of the third turn round, say "stop." Close and open your eyes quickly. After nine turns back, you should be able to recapture the moment. Nine is the number of completion. It is also the number of wish fulfillment. Watches and clocks are ruled by Saturn, who controls and keeps time. Turning a watch back can trigger the subconscious to go back in time. It is also a way of petitioning Saturn to manipulate time for us. The spell should end by burning a small white candle to stabilize the memory and add light to it so that the feeling or experience you want to recapture can live again in the present.

The second spell should begin with the burning of a white candle to heal the negative feelings or mood that has been created. Turn the clock or watch back to ten minutes before the problem began. Meditate and ask for another chance. When the clock returns to the exact time when things began to go wrong, walk around the room clockwise with the white candle. Do this three times. After the third round, place the candle on a table or altar and say: "Time time help me find a new beginning in this time." If the negative turn of events involved another person, this would be the time to forgive and make up and make the best of the time you have left. This spell does not substitute for an apology, but it does help to clear the air and banish anger and moodiness.

The third approach should be performed at the beginning of an evening. For example, suppose you have a date with someone special from 8 p.m. to midnight. The time is precious and you do not want it to fly by. At around 6 or 6:30, take your watch and set it at 8 p.m. Slowly turn it until it hits midnight. Slowly move the hour hand back to 8 p.m. Move the watch forward and back three times while chanting: "Time move like the turtle. Time crawl like the snail. Time please move slowly. Let the magic unveil.'' Leave the watch set at 10:00, the midpoint between the starting and finishing time. Light a white candle and let it burn next to the watch. This can be done before any important event to make sure that the time does not move too quickly.

SPELL FOR SERIOUS AND COMMITTED RELATIONSHIPS

Ingredients:

brown candles
cranberries or cranberry juice

Black and brown are the colors of Saturn. Many astrologers believe that people should not get married until after their Saturn Return, which occurs anywhere from the 28th to the 30th year of life, depending on the individual chart. It is believed that maturity and responsibility are learned and achieved after the transiting Saturn is conjunct with the natal Saturn.

Red is traditionally the color for deep abiding love. However, in the Amish tradition, the color brown is used in drawing or painting marriage hexes. Brown is used as the color to represent serious matters of love between two individuals. It is also believed by astrologers that when Saturn transits through the seventh house (house of marriage and partnerships), it can make or break a relationship. Saturn rules life and the length of a life, as well as the longevity of a relationship. Brown can certainly be used to cause quarrels or sever ties, but when offered as a devotional to Saturn, it can be used to empower and strengthen bonds.

Cranberries are used for magical protection and healing. They are also sacred to Saturn. The cranberry, because of its bitterness, is believed to drive out any evil forces that would come against the petitioner. Of course, also due to it, cranberry is sometimes used to sour relationships between couples. Both and the color brown can be manipulated for purposes of strength or destruct

To keep a couple bound together, use one brown candle and inscribe the name of both parties into the candle. Surround the candle with a circle of dried cranberries and light. Make sure the candle burns to completion without the circle of cranberries being broken.

To break up a relationship, obtain two brown candles and inscribe a separate name on each candle. Place the candles side by side and surround them with a circle of dried cranberries. Burn for nine minutes and then extinguish. On the second night, move the candles a few inches apart and relight for nine minutes. You will continue this ritual for nine nights. As you move the candles farther and farther apart, move them so the circle of cranberries is broken. By the ninth night, the candles should be far apart and the circle of cranberries should be scattered about.

Note: The second method of performing this spell is considered BLACK MAGIC!

SPELL FOR POWER

Ingredients:

hex nuts
paper
black rollerball pen

Hex nuts are usually found in the hardware store, but can also be found in mega supermarkets. Hex nuts are a wonderful modern witch's tool. Saturn rules the sign

ınd bolts of the zodiac. Metal, iron, and steel are sacred to
.esigned to summon power and achievement. It is recom-
the arts or politics. On a Saturday evening, lay out two to
e. Write your power requests on small scraps of paper. Black
or this work as black is the color of Saturn. I recommend a
pen, as wet ink is believed to hold more power than dry ink.
Roll up ___ f paper and place one inside the hub of each hex nut. Place
the hex nuts in a pocket or purse, and during the course of the evening hold them
in one hand and roll them together as you would a pair of dice. You can also
bounce the hex nuts back and forth from one hand to another, letting them clank
against one another. Use them as you would a worry stone, rosary, or worry dolls.
You can also feed problems to the hex nuts and clank them together to dispel the
problem. The action can be used to break an obstacle or to obtain a powerful desire.
It is recommended to combine the lunar influence into this spell and work on
removing obstacles during the waning moon, and use the waxing moon to draw
the power you desire.

SUNDAY EVENINGS

Sunday is ruled by the sun. The sun rules health, creativity, home, family, children, glory, riches, protection, and success. The sun also rules happiness between
couples. Although it is the traditional day of rest, these spells should keep you
busy on Sundays. The following are an assortment of Sunday spells using ingredients sacred to the sun. All spells can be performed at sunrise or sunset on a
Sunday.

FOR HEALTH

Ingredients:

> **sunflower seeds**
> **olive oil**
> **assorted fruits**

Roast sunflower seeds in olive oil and eat early Sunday evening to add more years to your life. To increase your health and energy, place your favorite fruit in the sun for one hour at sunrise on Sunday morning and once again an hour before sunset. This will charge the fruit with the healing and revitalizing energies of the sun. Eat the fruit after the sun goes down to infuse your body with solar strength.

FOR FERTILITY

Ingredients:

> **whole pumpkins**
> **olive oil**
> **honey**
> **yellow rice**

For fertility, rub whole pumpkins with olive oil and honey and offer them to the river goddess on a full moon. Rice is also believed to be a fertility food. Couples trying to conceive should eat yellow rice on a Sunday on or directly after a new moon to magically increase their chances for conception.

FOR GLORY

Ingredients:

> **bay leaves**
> **golden apples**

This spell is used to attain public adoration, fame, honors, popularity, or excellence in your field. Take six golden apples and slice them into a tub of warm water on a Sunday evening. Add six handfuls of crushed bay leaves. Enter the bath and rub the fruit and leaves around the entire body. Eat an apple slice and chew on a bay leaf while in the tub. This bath should be repeated every Sunday until you feel a change in your position. The bath is used to change your physical vibration and aura. It may take some time to work.

FOR RICHES

Ingredients:

> **saffron**
> **corn**
> **pineapple**

Corn is a staple food. It can draw prosperity on a spiritual level and keep one from poverty. Saffron and pineapple are extravagant foods of wealth. The combination of all three should draw long-lasting riches. This spell is very good to use for a growing business or to make long-term money through wise investments. Saffron is also known as a psychic spice and can be used to intuitively lead you to good fortune. Drink saffron tea and prepare a salad with corn kernels and pineapple slices. Eat on Sunday evenings during waxing moon periods.

FOR PROTECTION

Ingredients:

> **salt**
> **dried gourds**

Gourds hung around the house are believed to guard against evil. Salt sprinkled around a house or added to bath water is said to purify the home and body and protect against harm. Salt and gourds together give double protection. Add salt and gourds to your bath water or sprinkle coarse salt in a clockwise direction around the home and place gourds near all windows and doors.

FOR HAPPINESS BETWEEN COUPLES

Ingredients:

> **rosemary**
> **oranges**

honey
nutmeg

Rosemary and honey remind partners of the sweet memories that live between them. They are excellent to ingest when bad memories begin to creep in and take over the conscious mind. Oranges open the heart, and the combination of orange and nutmeg can help to regain trust and reawaken passion in a relationship. The combination of all four ingredients keeps the heart open, happy memories in the forefront, sweet experiences in the present, and a feeling of well-being and excitement about what the future may hold.

NEEDLES AND PINS

Needles and pins can easily be obtained at the supermarket; however, the magical use of such items requires great skill and wisdom. I have encountered numerous poppet spells gone tragically wrong. Even the most practiced of witches, virtual crones, have been known to shy away from needles and pins spells. In the end of this chapter, you will find some traditional methods of casting such spells, but I warn you: Proceed at your own risk.

In the meantime, here are two modern needles and pins spells that my coven sisters and I have found to be most safe and effective.

NEEDLES

Ingredients:

pine needles taken from a bed of earth in the forest or swept up from under your own Christmas tree.

Pine needles are sacred to the spirits of the woods. Aside from having great healing powers, they are known to ward off evil and to cleanse the spirit. According to eighteenth-century lore, chewing pine needles protected one from gunshot wounds. Also known as evergreen, pine is used to draw money and prosperity. To work this spell, take a handful of fresh pine needles and rub vigorously between the palms. Focus on your desire, be it protection, healing, cleansing, or prosperity. Feel the needles prick your palms, and as they do so, visualize your desire piercing into physical manifestation.

Complete the ritual as follows:

For healing, also rub the pine needles over the area of the body that needs healing.

For protection, place some pine needles in the mouth and chew.

For cleansing, add pine needles to bath water and soak, or, after rubbing in palms, pass your hands over your entire body. Begin at the top of the head and move down toward the feet. End by rubbing the soles of the feet.

For prosperity, after rubbing pine needles in palms fill your pockets or purse with crushed pine needles.

PINS

Ingredients:

bowling alley, bowling ball, and bowling pins

Laugh if you will, but my coven and I can often be found working spells at a particular bowling alley in upstate New York. It happens to reside right next to our favorite supermarket. When we bowl we are actually doing specific visualizations to create certain effects. This magic is known as tower magic. The idea is to break down anything in the way of achieving your goal. The goal may be of a positive or negative nature. For instance, you may want to get rid of an annoying situation (this would be a negative problem). As you view the pins, see each one as a representation of the problem and try to strike them all down. You may want to invoke a positive situation (e.g., to increase your earning power and financial status). Each pin will represent a hurdle in your path to success. Every pin you knock down represents a hurdle you can jump.

The game can become more complex, layered, and used as a form of divination by assigning an option or plan to each pin. Sometimes there are so many choices in life that we get bogged down by making decisions instead of fulfilling them. For example, you have ten possible choices to increase your income. Assign a choice to each pin. The ones knocked down first will be the easiest to fulfill. The ones left standing are the more difficult paths. Bowling a spare would indicate which issues to deal with initially (the first half of pins knocked down) and which choices represent more far-reaching goals (the second half of pins knocked down). If you bowl a strike, all paths lead to prosperity.

You can also use the game as a power tool. Whatever the objective, see the ball as an extension of your will and the pins as your goal. As the ball knocks down pins, your will is being strengthened in order to create physical change. By the way, the Witches League is known to have bowled 300 and won!

ZIP THE LIP SPELL

Ingredients:

> **gingerbread cookie**
> **scotch tape**
> **nine needles or pins**

I have never tried this spell myself (nor would I), but I overheard a certain witchlet bragging of its effects. It seems she was going to attend a certain party where a certain someone she adored was sure to show up. This party represented her big chance to get her claws into this guy. There was only one drawback: Her ex-boyfriend would also be attending the party. Or should I say, her loudmouth, braggart, revenge-seeking ex-boyfriend would also be attending this party. The witchlet was afraid he might ruin her reputation before she had a chance to turn on the charm.

The night before the party, she tossed and turned in bed wondering what to do. At midnight, she arose and wandered into the kitchen for some cookies and milk. As she indulged in her midnight snack, she absentmindedly took up a carving knife in her right hand. She stared down at the kitchen table and imagined her ex-boyfriend's face superimposed on the head of a gingerbread cookie. Anger rose in her gut; she raised the knife, about to strike off the cookie head. She stopped herself with a wicked cackle and thought out loud: "No, I don't want to kill him. I just want him to keep his mouth shut. Just keep his mouth shut,* and maybe I want to

---

Crone's note: A council of elders has determined that it was after this point that
the spell went awry. Remember, everything you do comes back at you!

make him suffer. Yes, suffer and rage with jealousy when he sees me flirting with this hot new guy.'' With that thought she delicately carved her ex-boyfriend's name into the cookie.

The witchlet rose from the table and took some scotch tape out of a drawer. She went into her sewing basket and removed five needles and four straight pins. She stretched some tape across the red candied mouth of the gingerbread cookie. She then stuck the needles and pins in a circle around the mouth for power and good measure. She finished her milk and slept soundly.

The following night, dressed to the nines, she went to the party. The ex-boyfriend was nowhere in sight. He had suddenly come down with a terrible case of strep throat and had to spend the night in bed. The new man took quite an interest in her that night. He asked her out again and they had gone on five or six successful dates by the time I heard this story. The witchlet was bragging of her great success with the spell. The ex-boyfriend had been shut up long enough for her to get a hold on her new man. He had just asked her to join him in the Bahamas for a week, and she felt the relationship was now sewn up.

Not quite. I understand the week of the trip, she had to have her wisdom teeth removed. She spent the week in bed barely being able to talk. It seems the two men ran into each other in the Bahamas that same week and had a little chat.

MIDNIGHT HEART SPELL

Ingredients:

> **paper or lace doilies**
> **needle or pin**
> **red marker**

This old witch's spell was traditionally performed with a cloth doll or poppet. Using paper or parchment for creating talismans became popular during the Inquisition because the evidence was easier and quicker to destroy if necessary. Modern witches employ paper or parchment for ease, and the ancient custom of burning the paper to hide the evidence has now become a way to empower the spell.

At midnight on a full moon, take a paper or lace doily and make a paper cutout doll. Draw a red heart on the left side of the torso. Write the name of the person you desire in the heart. Take a sterilized needle or straight pin and prick your ring finger. Smear your blood on the heart and then prick the heart by placing the needle through it. Burn the paper doll and imagine his or her heart burning for you. After the paper has finished burning, let the needle cool, and then pick it up. On the next full moon, place the pin or needle in a place where he or she is sure to see it. It is believed that if he or she picks it up, the spell will begin to take effect. If the needle or pin is not picked up, this person's heart genuinely belongs to another.

WITCH'S BOTTLE

Ingredients:

> needles and pins
> rusty nails
> broken pieces of mirror
> dried onion flakes
> cayenne pepper
> black pepper
> vinegar
> black candle

It is considered good luck to pick up needles and pins as well as coins from the street. Witches believe that a coin should only be picked up if it faces heads up. If the coin faces tails up, you should turn it over but not take it. It is customary and considered good karma to leave this heads-up lucky coin for someone else to pick up. (The rule of thumb with paper money is to pick it up as soon as possible, no matter which end is up.)

Needles and pins, including bobby pins, are even luckier than coins. However, I would caution against gathering hypodermic needles from off the street. Really, I am not kidding! This could be highly unlucky and very dangerous.

Witches have an old ritual that involves collecting pins, broken mirrors, rusty nails, and even tinfoil from streets and roads. The gathering should begin on a dark moon. (One day before the new moon.) Any sharp, rusty, jagged-edged, or reflective material is carefully picked up and stored in a jar. It is believed these materials can be used to impale demons or reflect away any negative energy that might come against the witch. It is very important to note that all these items must be found. Never break a mirror to collect broken pieces. This would be very unlucky. On the next dark moon, approximately 28 or 29 nights later, the jar is filled with baneful herbs. Many of these herbs cannot be found at the supermarket. Most are even illegal to sell in occult stores. The diehard witch will have to go out and gather these herbs herself in the wild. However, black and red (cayenne) pepper and onion are on the top ten of the baneful list. Their fiery burning natures can be used to ward off evil, and they can be found in the supermarket.

After adding the herbs, the jar is placed by the bed until morning. In the morning, the witch will urinate into the bottle and then fill it to the top with vinegar. It is said that the first urination of the day is the most potent, and there is nothing more potent than piss and vinegar! The jar is then sealed and placed in a safe place. At midnight the lid of the jar should be sealed with the wax of a black candle. Then the jar should be buried on the property or placed in the back of a dark cupboard or closet. The bottle should never be touched again unless a move occurs. If the bottle has been buried, it should be left in the ground and a new bottle created for the new home. If the bottle has been placed in a closet or cupboard, it should be disposed of properly when moving, and a new bottle created for the new home.

SLEEP TIGHT

BEDTIME SPELL

Ingredients:

> **poppy seed cake**
> **hot cocoa with honey**

This recipe can be served to children or anyone else whom you would like to put to bed before the evening gets going. I like to call it the "not seen and not heard spell." It actually works well on pets, too. However, if you are working the spell on a noisy, attention-seeking dog, please do not use cocoa or chocolate as this ingredient is very harmful to dogs.

Simply feed the precious and precocious party a spoonful of poppy seeds or poppy seed cake. Heat up some whole milk and stir in a teaspoon of honey and cocoa powder. As you stir in these ingredients, chant:

> *you are growing sleepy*
> *don't be weepy*
> *just get sleepy*

and when you go to sleep
let's not hear a peep
so mote it be

Serve this drink to your child, pet, husband, or whomever. Milk is known to produce sleepiness. Cocoa and honey will make the prospect of going to sleep appealing, even tantalizing. For there is nothing worse than a whining or belligerent child giving you a hard time while you are trying to time ten dishes in the oven. Or a smarmy black cat who thinks it is cute to rub up against you in your freshly pressed white suit. Not to mention a spouse who wants to stay up and go over the weekly household budget on your poker night with the gang!

Poppy brings sweet dreams, and combined with the other ingredients it will promote a long sleep with no disturbances in the middle of the night. This is especially helpful to avoid that midnight call for a glass of water just as you were about to serve your crème brûlée à la flambeau.

SILENT NIGHT SPELL

(to banish noisy neighbors)

This spell is for the enchanted evening that consists of a *quiet* night at home alone. Perhaps you just want to read or meditate or have a serious and thoughtful conversation with one you love. Maybe you have a business meeting with a very important prospective client. Whatever the plan, it's impossible to concentrate with that horrid techno music they are blasting next door. I have found this spell most effective for banishing noise pollution and the people who produce it.

Ingredients:

> **gray candle**
> **coarse salt**
> **sharp knife or pin**

Gray is the color to neutralize situations. It can also be used to banish noise. Obtain a gray candle and carve the name of the offensive parties or offensive situation onto the face of the candle. Place a circle of coarse salt around the candle. Salt is also used to neutralize a situation. As you light the candle, chant three times: ''I banish you. I banish you. I banish you.'' (Name the people or disturbing situation they are creating.) ''Go back go back go back from whence ye came.'' Try to summon up as much energy as you can while chanting. Get as angry and as loud, or as deadly silent as you need to. Once the candle is lit and the chant is completed, you can continue to visualize the problem disappearing. However, when the candle finishes burning, let go of the situation. Do not dwell on it. Ignore it and let the magic take over. After the candle has gone out (I suggest you use as small a candle as possible so that this ritual does not take you all night to perform), roll up the remaining wax with the salt and store in a dark cupboard. On the dark moon you can bury the wax ball to permanently rid yourself of the problem.

Note: This spell is quite effective; however, you must be somewhat realistic with your magical intent. A friend of mine in East Berlin reported many unsuccessful results while performing this spell. At the time he was living right next door to the largest construction site in the world. His apartment was extremely noisy from eight to eighteen hundred hours. After the twentieth failed attempt, just as he thought he would lose his mind, he discovered that the great mound of salted wax he had accumulated could be fashioned into great ear plugs. Ah so, his problem was solved after all.

SPELL FOR A GOOD NIGHT'S SLEEP

Ingredients:

linden flowers or linden tea
lavender flowers or lavender soap
poppy seeds
pomegranate seeds
star anise

These ingredients should be sewn up in a silk bag or folded up in tissue paper and placed under the pillow or mattress. Nineteenth-century herbalists would prescribe a mixture of linden and lavender to cure insomnia. Poppy seeds and star anise stimulate the subconscious and draw us into the dream world. Combined with pomegranate, the infamous seed swallowed by Persephone to lead her into the underworld, the sleep will be of the deepest nature possible. Placed under the pillow, this potion works with the principles of aromatherapy. The smelling of this herbal recipe will subtly affect the body and bring the deepest state of relaxation, thus leading you into a good night's sleep.

NIGHTMARE SPELL

Ingredients:

eucalyptus
flax or linseed

salt
chamomile (optional)

Flax or linseed is used to make linen cloth, so if your sheets are linen, you are already set. Although flax is most often used in money and healing spells, there are many medieval references to using flax around the bedside to ward off evil. Eucalyptus is also used primarily for healing, but it is a strong repellent to evil spirits or any form of disease. Lift up your mattress and sprinkle a handful of flax seeds and eucalyptus leaves underneath. If you are experiencing nightmares add a pinch of coarse salt. For insomnia add a pinch of chamomile.

SPELL TO ENCHANT YOUR DREAMS

Ingredients:

vanilla
licorice
marshmallow

It might be kind of messy to put these three items under the pillow. Try eating a marshmallow and a licorice stick before bedtime and place a vanilla bean under your pillow. You can also substitute star anise or anise for licorice. All are sacred to Neptune and are believed to lead one into a magical dream land. Vanilla is a sex bean, but combined with anise it brings happiness. (It is also alleged to make love dreams come true.) Marshmallow is used to attract friendly spirits and is also believed to make one sleepy.

For best results, rub a dab of vanilla extract on a marshmallow and stuff a piece of licorice inside. Eat the marshmallow right before falling asleep. Sweet dreams.

SEASONS OF THE WITCH

In pagan lore there are certain magical foods and plants associated with each season. If you are planning a party, use these foods to invoke the blessings of that particular cycle of the year.

AUTUMN PARTIES

Ingredients:

- corn
- pomegranates
- pumpkins
- squash
- spicy foods
- apples

Autumn is the time of the harvest. Corn is one of the most sacred symbols of the harvest. It represents fertility, prosperity, and good health. Hang colored corn around the room at an autumn party to invoke a bountiful mood. You can also serve corn to guests. White or snow queen corn is best if you are trying to sweeten people up or form new relationships. Yellow corn is eaten to culminate deals or to bring out the fullness of relationships. Corn served with salted butter is best for business matters. Corn served with sweet unsalted butter is good for emotional ties. Corn roasted in toasted sesame oil is used for opening up sexual channels.

The pomegranate has a myriad of symbolism depending upon which culture you examine. In Middle Eastern tradition, it represents prosperity. In Greek lore, it is the food of female power and mystery. Fill a bowl with pomegranates for decoration at a party. If you want to create an air of mystery and daring, slice them open and serve.

Squash and pumpkin are sacred to Oshun. Oshun is an African/Cuban goddess similar to Venus. She resides over gold and love. It is customary not to eat pumpkin when you work with Oshun, but rather to prepare the pumpkin as an offering to the goddess. Take a whole pumpkin and spray paint it gold. Place it on a table and surround it with chocolate coins wrapped in gold foil. With this as a centerpiece, you are sure to hold a successful business party. If the party is of a more romantic nature, hollow out the pumpkins first. Then spray paint them copper. Fill the inside with chocolate kisses. Let the party guests pull the kisses out of the pumpkin for luck in love. In Native American and European lore, the pumpkin is eaten for prosperity or fertility. Spiced pumpkin is said to make wishes come true. If you are making a pumpkin pie, make wishes for your party as you stir in the nutmeg and allspice. You can also tell your guests to make wishes of their own as they eat the pie. Jack-o-lanterns were believed to scare away ghosts on Halloween. Scary faces were carved into the hollowed pumpkins and then candles were lit inside. You can make Jack-o-lanterns to protect your party from harmful forces. Witches actually use Jack-o-lanterns to draw good spirits to their rites. They are still used for protection, but the idea is to draw friendly protective forces as opposed to banishing negative forces. Witches believe that if a space is filled with white light and positive energy, there is no room for any other force to enter.

All spicy foods are sacred to the fall season. They warm the blood and prepare the body for the oncoming cold. They also prepare the body for change and help us to think and move quickly. Autumn is traditionally the time of death or change. The pace quickens as winter hastens. Serving spicy foods will give your guests energy and bless them with stamina to survive the cold months ahead.

Apples can be eaten any time of year, but when eaten in the fall, they bring special blessings. The apple is the fruit of the goddess and represents her creative power. Hidden within the apple is the pentagram, sacred symbol of the witches. If you cut an apple in half horizontally you will find the five-pointed star. It is believed that looking at the star and then taking a bite between the autumn equinox and Samhain (Halloween) will bring blessings the whole year long. If you serve candied apples to your guests, their year will be full of sweetness.

WINTER PARTIES

Ingredients:

holly
laurel wreaths or bay leaves
pine

colored lights or candles
wine, ale, or beer
cinnamon sticks
cloves
allspice
nutmeg
beets
vinegar
red cabbage
apples
ham or roast pork
honey
pineapple
mistletoe
chestnuts

Most of the traditional decorations for Christmas are actually remnants of ancient pagan customs. They were used to celebrate the winter solstice and Saturnalia. The holly and laurel were believed to bring protection and luck into the home all winter long. Evergreen or pine was a symbol of the god of the woods or nature. Tradition held that at the end of winter all these items must be burned in order to summon in the spring. In today's world we see trees and wreaths being dumped on the street beginning the day after Christmas. The ancient pagans kept these branches on the hearth all winter long. The stem of the tree, or Yule log, was even saved a whole year and burned on the following solstice for continuity of the gods' blessings. Bright and colorful candles or lights were lit to welcome the birth of the Sun god. Use these traditional Yuletide decorations with the added knowledge that they are bringing protection, luck, life, and light into your home.

Wassail is a special drink served on the winter solstice. Originally the word was used as a drinking salute meaning "be whole" or "to your health." Later on it came to also represent the liquor used to make the toast. A traditional recipe is to mull wine or ale or beer with cinnamon sticks, cloves, allspice and nutmeg. This brew is said to bestow health and blessings on all who drink it. If wassail is made with beer or ale it adds extra protection. If prepared with wine, it enhances your power of divination.

Prepare a beet salad by peeling beets and boiling for seven to ten minutes. You want the beets to remain al dente, so they don't lose their vitamins and minerals. Let beets cool by running them under cold water. Slice thin and mix with olive oil, tarragon vinegar, and salt and pepper to taste. Beets and vinegar are ruled by Saturn. Beets bring power and longevity. Vinegar is a cleanser. Olive oil invokes the warmth of the sun and is added for good health. Tarragon, salt, and pepper are also used for purification and health.

A nice complement to the beet salad is a red cabbage salad with chopped apples. Shred and steam red cabbage, then add diced apples and honey to taste. Red cabbage is also ruled by Saturn and said to keep one healthy and robust. Honey and apples are sacred to Ops, the wife of Saturn. She is the goddess of plenty. This sweeter salad should be eaten after the cleansing beet salad to bless yourself and loved ones with happiness, good health, and stamina throughout the winter months.

Catholics believe that eating the host is symbolic of eating the body of Christ. The ancient pagans believed the energy of the dying god was represented by a slaughtered pig or boar. The eating of this meat would summon the rebirth of the god in each individual. Roast pork or ham should be prepared by glazing the meat with honey, then either stuffing or garnishing the meat with pineapple and apples. This lends the nurturing aspect of the goddess to the sacrificed god.

Mistletoe was believed to bring luck to the hunter. During the winter months when vegetation was sparse, the successful hunting of meat meant survival. Mistletoe is also used for another type of hunt. If you want to pierce someone with Cupid's arrow, kiss him/her under the mistletoe. Be careful, though; mistletoe is also believed to promote conception. Hang over the bed to increase fertility.

Last but not least, roasting chestnuts over an open fire (or even in the oven) is said to increase your luck in love. Serve these at more intimate gatherings.

Duck Duck Goose

Ingredients:

goose

Remember the childhood game Duck Duck Goose? Everyone would sit in a circle, one child would walk around the circle patting the top of each head while calling "Duck, duck, duck," and whenever he or she felt inclined, the word "goose" would emerge from the lips. As though lightning had struck, the head that had been touched on the word "goose" would pop up to give chase to the caller. If the caller was able to sit in the empty space in the circle before being tagged, the goose would become the new caller. If the caller was tagged before sitting, he or she would remain the caller. To be tagged as "goose" was the same as saying "you're it!" Although most children feared the "it," there is no denying the electrical and awe-inspiring charge of being the chosen one.

It is no coincidence that duck represents the normal population while goose represents the other; the one *chosen* for a special calling. After all, it was a goose who laid the golden egg. Geese are very magical birds surrounded by mythology and folklore. The goose was sacred to the ancient Celtic tribes, and in Egyptian lore, the goose was the goddess Hathor, who gave birth to the sun (the golden egg). In pre–Christian times, it was taboo to eat goose during the winter months. The pagans believed the goose's maternal energy needed to be kept alive in order to nurture and strengthen the newborn sun. Eventually the custom reversed itself, and goose became a very traditional Christmas or Yule dish. Modern carnivorous pagans accept the new custom and believe that by eating goose, the goddess will nurture the individual soul (or sun within) during the winter months. Modern vegan witches stick with the old tradition and prefer to leave the goose alive. If you are lucky enough to see a flock of wild geese migrating, you should consider yourself blessed. As they fly overhead, pray for spiritual nurturing and strength.

If you eat goose, you should do so only on a sacred event or holiday such as Yule, Christmas, or New Year's. Eating goose will prepare you for a challenging spiritual task. If you feel you have already been chosen, eat goose to make sure you live up to the assignment. Eating goose can also increase your awareness of the Divine and bring forth both spiritual and material bounty. If you eat goose more than three times in one year, others will be in awe of you and your spiritual powers.

SPRING PARTIES

Ingredients:

> **daisies**
> **snapdragons**
> **eggs**
> **rhubarb**

artichokes
fennel

All spring flowers add life and vibrancy to a party. Daises restore innocence, and snapdragons invoke mischief and discovery. Eggs bring rebirth and creativity. Deviled eggs can revive the sex drive. Rhubarb is ruled by Venus but also falls under the sign of Aries. The spring equinox is marked by the sun entering the sign of Aries. Rhubarb is a zesty love food with a bite. It is excellent to serve at spring parties and will make people come out of their shells quickly and be more bold in expressing friendship, lust, and love. The artichoke is eaten for beauty and protection. It can help people feel safe enough to reveal their inner beauty. Not a food to serve if you and your guests like to put on airs. Fennel is a psychic and spiritual cleanser. It helps us to shed the heaviness of winter. It is also a Mercurial food and helps promote clever conversation. Serve fennel for laughter, lightness, and gaiety.

SUMMER PARTIES

Ingredients:

watermelon
summer fruits
berries
coconut, mango, papaya
crab, shellfish
croissants
cucumber yogurt salad
avocado and shrimp salad

All berries bring protection. Melon and plums create sexual energy. Fruit salad with sunflower seeds bring prosperity. Coconut, mango, and papaya served together with crab meat can bless a home and its inhabitants. Coconut cleanses and removes obstacles. Mango and papaya are fruits of fertility and love. Eaten alone they produce feelings of lust, but tempered with coconut they act more as joyful conductors of light and fun. Crab meat is sacred to the moon and the sign of Cancer. The summer solstice is marked by the sun moving into the sign of Cancer. Crab meat can be eaten to create a stronger bond with home or family members. If you are looking to expand your dwelling eat this salad for luck in finding a bigger home. It can also be eaten to increase the bonds within the home and between members of the household.

In Ecuador there is a special ritual of eating avocado and shrimp salad. Prepare the salad with fresh steamed shrimp, sliced avocado, mayonnaise, lemon, and a pinch of salt. It is believed that eating this salad will reveal the inner beauty of the soul and help to attract your one true soul mate.

Cucumbers and yogurt are both ruled by the moon and are said to be foods of protection and psychic inducers. It is also believed that introducing these foods into the body will help prevent sun poisoning or any kind of sickness from over-exposure to the sun.

Eating croissants in the summer months, especially on the eve of the summer solstice or on any new moon during the summer months, is believed to make wishes come true.

Note: The following dates are the eight most enchanted evenings of the year. These are the Witches Sabbats. I could write a whole book (and I probably will) on how to celebrate these evenings. But for now, just mark the dates and celebrate by honoring the god and goddess in the best way you know how.

October 31—Samhain or the Witches New Year
December 20–23*—Winter Solstice
February 1—Candlemas or Brigid's Day or Imbolc
March 21–23**—Spring Equinox
May 1—Beltane or May Day
June 21–23†—Summer Solstice
August 1—Lammas or Lughnasad
September 21–23‡—Autumn Equinox

*Date varies each year. The winter solstice is marked by the sun entering Capricorn.
**Date varies each year. The spring equinox is marked by the sun entering Aries.
†Date varies each year. The summer solstice is marked by the sun entering Cancer.
‡Date varies each year. The autumn equinox is marked by the sun entering Libra.

Home Alone

SELF IMAGE OR CONFIDENCE SPELL

Ingredients:

    black shoe polish
    clean white cloth
    pair of shoes
    spit

It was actually the arrival of the First and Second World Wars that made shoe polish a popular and common product. With all the pomp and circumstance of war, there was a great demand for shoe polish among the soldiers. When they returned home, they introduced the product into their households. The properties of shoe polish would make it sacred to the Roman god Vulcan, the vulgar forger of tools. Vulcan was originally petitioned to ward off the destructive element of fire. Vulcan can help us burn off the fires of self-hatred or self-rage that burn within us. He can help us to melt down these fires and forge them into self-confidence, a necessary tool for success.

The color white represents cleansing and healing. Aside from having a very functional purpose in this spell, white cloth is used in the most sacred of rituals as an altar covering. It is said to attract angelic and friendly spirits who will lend power to the spell.

Shoes keep us connected to the ground and they also lead the way into the world. Many cultures have lore surrounding shoes. Native Americans believe you should not judge someone until you have walked a mile in his or her shoes. There is a Jewish taboo against wearing the shoes of a dead person. "If the shoe fits, wear it" and "put your best foot forward" are both popular modern sayings. Shoes are tools of power and represent leadership.

Spit is one of the most magical forms of body fluid. It can be used to either change or bind things. This spell will begin by changing your self-image from negative to positive. It will end by binding the positive reinforcement.

Think of your shoes as a sacred tool or altar. They are the magical tools or altars that lead you through life. Cover your shoes with a clean white cloth. Bless the shoes and ask them to lead you down a strong and confident path. Using a brush, spread black* shoe polish on the shoes. As you do so, visualize all your insecurities. Spit on the shoes and begin to polish them with the white cloth. As you do so, imagine all this negative imagery being transformed. Visualize all the qualities of self-confidence that you would like to possess. When your visualization is strong and the shoes have been finely polished, step into the shoes. Feel and imagine all the new and shiny qualities rising up through the shoes, entering into your feet, and spreading up your entire body. Once you feel the energy rise to the top of your head, put your right foot forward and loudly and confidently call out your

*Black is the strongest color to use for removing negative energy. Second-best colors would be white or tan. Please make sure your shoes match the color you choose to use!

full name three times. The spell has now been completed. Witches believe that once a tool has been consecrated, it should be used immediately. Keep your shoes on and do something confidently.

SAFE HOME SPELL

Ingredients:

peppermint
wintergreen
chamomile
cucumber

Peppermint and wintergreen are used to protect the inside of a dwelling. Chamomile is used to protect the outside. I added cucumber to this traditional blend for a client who never went out because she was too nervous about someone breaking into her home. Cucumber is sacred to Yemeya, the household goddess. It is used to protect and bless a home. Cucumber and chamomile combined not only bring peaceful vibrations into the home, they also relax the home owner or dweller.

Fill a pot with spring water or holy water.* Add three chamomile tea bags and the skin of a cucumber. Bring the brew to a boil, cover, and simmer for ten minutes. Take the pot off the stove and allow the water to cool. Obtain a spray bottle and pour contents from pot into bottle. Spray a light mist around the outside of your home. Start at the front door and walk around in a clockwise direction until you

*I understand you can purchase holy water at the local supermarket in Lourdes, France, as well as Fatima, Portugal.

have come full circle. Continue the ritual by generously spraying the outside of all doors and vulnerable window frames. Mist keyholes inside and out.

If you live in an apartment building, you do not need to walk around the whole structure and mist. Simply spray all your doors, windows, and keyholes. You might want to mist the main entrance and vestibule of the building as well, to keep you safe as you are coming and going.

Complete the ritual by sprinkling crushed or powdered peppermint and wintergreen leaves in the four corners of each room. Begin in the east and move around in a clockwise direction until you have come full circle. Now go out and have a good time. Or relax and get a good night's sleep. Don't worry, your home will be protected.*

For added peace of mind, drink a cup of chamomile tea and eat a slice of cucumber.

GET OFF MY PROPERTY SPELL

Ingredients:

> **sea salt**
> **bay leaves**
> **red wine**
> **cinnamon**
> **turnips**

---

*Witch's clause: Your home will be protected provided you take the standard earth plane precautions such as locking your door, windows, turning on the alarm, etc.

This is an old banishing formula used by witches. Salt and wine are used to purify and sanctify an area. Turnips repel negative energy. Bay and cinnamon bring speedy success to any ritual. It is used to banish people loitering on your property.

You will begin by blending a mixture of equal parts sea salt, crushed bay leaves, cinnamon powder, and turnip shavings. Add a teaspoon of red wine and mix in a bowl. Sprinkle the mixture on the stoop of your building, sidewalk, or anywhere on the property where people are loitering. Make sure to do this at an hour when no one is present. This spell is most effective when performed on a waning or dark moon. You can also sprinkle the blend inside the home to banish feelings of unrest, anxiety, anger, or any form of negative energy.

JAMMIN JELL-O SPELLS

Ingredients:

fruit-flavored gelatin (all colors and flavors) and various other ingredients

Right up there with apple pie, "the jiggly dish" is considered America's favorite dessert. According to the electroencephalograph exhibit in the Jell-O museum in Le Roy, New York, gelatin produces almost the exact same waves as the human brain.* Food for thought, and magic. Serve fruit flavored gelatin dishes as a dessert to create specific cerebral conditions.

Let's begin with the happiness and health of your children. Choose a cherry-flavored gelatin and add sunflower seeds before the mold completely sets. Serve

---

*William Glaberson, "Celebrating a Jiggly Dessert's Place in History," *New York Times*, 27 July 1997.

to the whole family with a Sunday supper to promote self-confidence and to open up your kids to sharing their thoughts with you. Sunflower seeds are believed to prevent illness, so this dish is exceptionally good if you are afraid your children may be coming down with something. This recipe will also set a fun and confident mood for the kids and can be served any time you want to spend an evening with them.

Lemon gelatin with blueberries can be served if you feel you need any kind of protection during the evening. Perhaps you are alone in the house and afraid of being burglarized. Maybe you know you will be in some kind of negative situation that night. Blueberries protect the physical and emotional body. They also drive away evil. Lemon is used to purify and cleanse. Lemon can remove negative obstacles or harm from your path.

Lime-flavored gelatin with orange slices can create an evening of power and sexuality. Use to influence a reluctant partner into a romantic liaison.

Eat strawberry-flavored gelatin with kiwi slices to create more trust and understanding between partners. Strawberry-flavored gelatin with orange and banana slices can bless a marriage and help solve domestic problems. All these fruits are sacred to the Haitian deity Erzuli. She presides over love and marriage.

To create more money-making incentive and to improve sales, serve mint-flavored gelatin with celery and walnuts to your employees. You can serve lime gelatin with celery and walnuts to an employer to influence him or her to give you a raise or promotion. Eat lime gelatin with parsley and walnuts to increase your own earning power or to help in the search for employment.

Lemon-lime gelatin should be used to remove obstacles from your path. It is also a good spiritual cleanser. Add a quarter teaspoon of rose water to lemon-lime gelatin to remove obstacles in your romantic life.

ENCHANTED ELEPHANT SPELL

Ingredients:

one dozen elephants
or **jasmine and ginseng tea and perfume and sandals**

Elephants are magnificent and sacred beasts. In the Old Testament, the elephant is referred to as the Behemoth. The behemoth was demonized in the later culture, but it was worshipped by the original Hebrews as one aspect of the godhead. The Indian God Ganesh is represented by an elephant. Ganesh is the god of good fortune, wisdom, and literature. He is also the remover of obstacles. It is said if an elephant crosses your path, all your bad luck will disappear.

Every spring the circus comes to town, and when it does, it marches the elephants on foot through the Manhattan Midtown tunnel. It is quite a sight to see. A group of us were convinced that witnessing this event would magically remove the obstacles from our lives. The group comprised my dear friends Omar, Olivia, Alexandar, César, and myself. We all had our share of misfortune at the time. Olivia and Omar were stressed out from work and desperately needed some quality time together. Alexandar had just returned from Paris broken-hearted. It seems the woman he believed to be his soul mate had dumped him. She went back to her husband after he made a miraculous recovery and broke all medical records by returning from the dead. César, an unemployed dancer, had been in and out of a sickbed all winter. He was stir-crazy and creatively frustrated. My muses had left me at a serious roadblock in my writing. I also couldn't afford to renew my lease and was about to become homeless. Having a dozen or so elephants cross our path seemed like a suitable remedy. I also suspected that watching them emerge from the tunnel would help us to tunnel or plow through our problems with the strength of the mighty behemoth.

On the appointed night we all gathered except for César, who felt too poorly to leave his bed that night. I, myself, was in a sulfur and brimstone mood. Omar and Olivia were very quiet, and I believe they may have been quarreling on the way over. Alex, as usual, was distracted and beside himself. I have come to the conclusion that Alex's problem is not really women. It is his vision. He never seems to have a clear picture about who it is he's getting involved with and why. Alex is always examining everything. Things that don't need examining. Things that are apparent to the naked eye. He goes over and over the small details of life and never seems to get the big picture. I hoped at least the elephants might broaden his view.

Traffic was blocked off on the east side of 34th Street. At around twenty-three hundred hours, the elephants emerged from the tunnel and came into view. All of our moods were immediately transformed by this majestic sight. I spied Omar and Olivia reaching for each other's hands. I reached over to wrap my arm around Alex's shoulder.

"God what a gray and foggy night. Do you see them yet?" asked Alex.

I took my eyes off the beautiful beasts for a moment, astonished to see what Alex was up to.

"Alex, do you really think you need those binoculars to see twenty elephants marching up the street two feet in front of your nose?" sneered Olivia.

"Oh," he exclaimed in a daze, "I hadn't thought about that. I wanted to bring my camera but it was too bulky. I thought the binoculars would be easier to carry. Besides, my life is hardly worthy of a Kodak moment."

I gently pulled the field glass from his eye and watched true elation spread across his face. We ran with the elephants all the way to Madison Square Garden. We whispered our prayers their way, thanked them for their beauty and blessing, and then we all walked home.

Meanwhile, poor César was propped up in bed, drinking cups of jasmine and ginseng tea to clear his sinuses. His room was stuffy but he was afraid to open the windows because of the draft. Frustrated, he lay in bed with a perfume atomizer and sprayed the fragrance continually across his nose. Finally, he fell asleep in his leather sandals with the perfume atomizer still clutched in his hands. He dreamed of a company of elephants dancing a ballet through an obstacle course. They knocked down several barriers with some high kicks, and as they passed him, each elephant waved its trunk with a *relevé* and a turn.

Interestingly enough, jasmine and ginseng are the fragrances sacred to Ganesh. His magical weapons are perfume and sandals. If a magician wanted to summon the god, these are the tools needed to attract his attention.

I am happy to report that within two weeks of the Enchanted Elephant evening, Omar and Olivia both got time off from their jobs and planned a fabulous healing vacation together by the Portuguese seaside. I began to write again and got another book deal. I also found and moved into the most beautiful and affordable home I could ever have imagined. Alex met a new woman who is completely suited to him. Maria is from South America but Alex met her right in front of his apartment building. They are now engaged to be married, and Maria bought Alex a fabulous camera the size of a cigarette box. He carries it everywhere he goes to capture all the wonderful moments of his life and then looks back at them wistfully. César was finally able to *relever de maladie,** and he has packed his trunk to go on the road, dancing.

*get back on one's feet (after an illness)

DEMONS OF THE NIGHT

This section deals with all sorts of harmful situations that may occur at night.

THE JUST SAY NO SPELL

Ingredients:

peanut butter
mustard seeds (or powder)
a sneaker

Most of us know that the old adage of a former first lady just won't cut the mustard when it comes to drugs. This spell is designed to protect your children from the dangers and temptations of drugs. A little magic can go a long way when coupled with education and physical protection. Although this threat can be present at any hour of day or night, it is recommended to perform the spell before your child goes out in the early or late evening. The hours without sunlight are considered the most threatening hours, as we are governed by the moon and our subconscious mind, as opposed to daylight when we are ruled by the sun and our rational conscious minds. If the spell is set in motion at night, it will continue to protect your child during the day.

Take the right sneaker or running shoe of your child and pour a handful of mustard seeds (or powder) into the shoe. Roll them around in the shoe and visualize your child being rational and disciplined and staying drug-free. Roll out a piece of tinfoil on a counter and empty the mustard seeds onto the foil. Take a knife and spread a layer of peanut butter (smooth is preferred to crunchy) over the seeds on the tinfoil. Take the shoe in your right hand and make a shoe print in the peanut butter. Take the shoe and wipe it off with a paper towel. Try to leave a small remnant of the peanut butter and mustard seed (or powder) in the grooves of the shoe. Fold up the tinfoil into a small square and keep as a protective talisman for your child. You can place it in a drawer or behind a picture of the child. You can even place it in a pocket and rub all night if you are the type of parent prone to staying up all night and worrying until your child comes home.

Mustard seeds or powder help direct the actions of a person. Peanut butter grounds and protects. Shoes are considered symbolic of our path in life. Tin or aluminum foil is an attractant. In this case we are using it to attract positive direction, clarity, and grounding into your child's life.

ANTI-MUGGER SPELL

Ingredients:

> ginger
> lemon
> mint

There is a very magical herb called lo john root or galangal. It is very popular among witches and known to stop thieves. It is possible to obtain galangal root or powder in an occult shop or a very good herb store. Galangal is a cousin to the ginger plant and they have many similar properties. If you cannot obtain galangal, feel free to substitute ginger root or ginger powder. Ginger combined with mint puts a strong Martian glow in your aura that says "back off."

If you were to combine rose with mint and ginger you would have a love attraction formula, but when you add lemon, it becomes a protection and a repellent from any form of danger. I would compare the different energies with these images: The formula with rose is like wearing a fiery red dress, very tight and very low cut. The formula with lemon is like wearing an iron maiden with thorns protruding from its face.

Mix dried lemon peel, ginger root or powder, and fresh or dried mint in a bowl. Dust your hands, pockets, purse, or bag before going out at night. You can also dust your feet or tips of your shoes for added protection if you have to walk in a dangerous area that night.

SPELL FOR REMOVING ENVY AND JEALOUSY

Ingredients:

raw steak
cocoa butter
eggshells
cigar
white dish towel

brown paper bag
four pennies

This spell is very effective for removing envy and jealousy. There are moments in life when one must step out in front. This spell is used to protect yourself from those have nots who would seek to destroy your enchanted evening by placing the evil eye on you. The spell must be performed on a Thursday night. A Thursday that falls on or shortly after the new moon is best. This spell is used to ask for the blessing and protection of Obatala. S/he is considered the highest and purest of all the Yoruban deities. Obatala's day is Thursday, and all ingredients in this spell are sacred to Obatala.

Take a raw piece of meat and rub completely with cocoa butter and crushed eggshells. Light a cigar and carefully place the lit end in your mouth. (In my youth we would call this "shotgunning.") Blow smoke over the entire steak. Roll up the meat in white fabric and pass across your whole body from top to bottom. This should be done naked. Dress yourself afterward and place the cloth with meat in a paper bag. Place four pennies in the bag. Fold up the bag and throw out in the trash outside of your house. In the olden days the meat was thrown in the street where an old stray dog might eat it. The dog would then take your troubles away.

DANGEROUS LIAISON SPELL

Ingredients:

parsley
sage
rosemary

thyme
vinegar

Dating can be a war zone. This spell can be used in a variety of ways. If you have already made a dangerous liaison with someone and wish to end it, prepare a bottle with parsley flakes, sage, rosemary, and thyme. Fill the bottle with white vinegar. Add the name of the Glenn Close look-alike to the bottle. Shake the bottle every time this person calls or stalks you. Shake it every night before you go out to alleviate the fear as well as the actuality of running into him or her. Keep shaking the bottle until you are free and clear of this person.

The second way to use the formula is to avoid meeting someone who will ultimately become dangerous for you to become involved with. In this case, fill a small mixing bowl with all four herbs and add a teaspoon of vinegar. Stir seven times clockwise and six times counterclockwise. Run the bowl under your nose and sniff the ingredients before you go out cruising. If at any time during the evening you experience a sense memory of this smell, you will know that the person you are talking to is a potential problem. Keep away. Remember, an ounce of prevention is worth a pound of cure.

The third way to utilize the spell is for those with weak instincts. In this case you will fill a zipper-lock bag with all four herbs and two drops of vinegar. Seal the bag and carry with you during the evening. The bag will act as a repellent to potential loony tunes. They will not come near you.

All these herbs are known for their qualities of protection. Parsley is very Mercurial and is known as the great communicator. It is an informant of the highest caliber. The James Bond of the herbal spy world, parsley can feed you information on a psychic level. Sage is a purifier and an herb of wisdom. Sage can give you the wisdom to see what's beyond your chemical attraction to someone. Rosemary helps us remember things (e.g., don't get yourself in trouble again). Rosemary can also help us break destructive patterns. If you have a habit of getting involved in destructive relationships, rosemary can help you remember your mistakes and assist you in changing your patterns. Thyme is used in love spells to bring relationships that are satisfying to both parties. Use it to invoke a partner who will fulfill you, not terrorize you. Vinegar is a cleansing agent that wards off evil, harmful, and destructive influence. Vinegar is also used to strengthen and bind together all other ingredients of the spell.

FRAU KAUFMANN SPELL

Ingredients:

baby powder
sage
white pepper
arrowroot
white flour
three white eggshells

Frau Kaufmann was born in Colombia. She has recently taken up residence in Berlin, yet you will find Frau Kaufmann all over the world. She travels in the most dangerous of circles and is the most tempting of seductresses. She insinuates herself into unsuspecting lives with the charm and grace of a viper in kitten's clothing. She always dresses in white, but vampire red is her favorite color, as she is always out for blood, and she has the blackest of hearts.

Frau Kaufmann represents, no, Frau Kaufmann is, all that is evil in the world. Perhaps I am exaggerating. Let's just say that Frau K. is intrinsically connected with all that is evil in the world. Of this, I am quite sure. You will find her at every party, every opening, every street corner, lurking in the heart of every desperate and unsure human soul. She is a metaphor for all that you fear and all that tempts you. If there is something you know you should not do, or somewhere you know you should not go, or someone you know you should not meet, Frau Kaufmann will convince you that it is safe and fun and in fact a necessity to do just this very thing. She will promise to stand by and hold your hand. Then she will inevitably abandon you when the going gets tough. She will rob you of all your money, friends and loved ones. She will even rob you of your soul if you let her. Given enough time and access Frau Kaufmann can destroy even the best of us. A sly fox, she does not take no for an answer. She knows everyone's Achilles heel. Do not think that you can escape her charms without magical protection.

Here is the spell to ward off Frau Kaufmann, whomever or whatever she may represent to you. Take a white bowl and mix equal portions of baby powder, white sage powder, white pepper, arrowroot, and white flour. Pulverize three dry and clean white eggshells and add to the mixture. Sage and flour were used in Native American rituals for purification, protection, and to drive away the forces of evil. Arrowroot is used by witches to uncross or to remove negative obstacles from one's path. White pepper is used to repel hidden enemies. It can also be used to drive away those harmful energies that you are also attracted to. Eggshells, because they hold embryos, are considered sacred vessels of life. They emit a very strong spiritual vibration, and similar to the lore of vampires and garlic, evil spirits cannot tolerate the presence of eggshells. Baby powder or talc is used to bind all the ingredients together. Witches will often use a white or colored talc as a base to blend other important ingredients.

After mixing all ingredients, sprinkle in a circle on the floor. Stand in the middle of this circle and pray for protection. Witches perform very powerful rituals within such circles. There is a tradition of creating magical chalks or powders, such as this one, to draw sacred circles, in order to exorcise demons. After you have finished praying, gather some of the powder in your hands (do this without breaking the line of the circle) and dust your hands and feet for added protection. Frau Kaüfmann and her kind will steer clear of you after completing this ritual.

You should stand in the chalk circle for a minimum of twenty minutes. After dusting the hands and feet, you may step outside the circle and then sweep or vacuum it up. If you feel that Frau K. is hot on your heels, you may leave the circle intact for up to three days, and step inside whenever you feel her threatening presence. After sweeping up the circle, you may also sprinkle some powder across the threshold of your dwelling to keep Frau K. away.

HARD AND HECTIC NIGHTS

ANTI-ANXIETY SPELL

Ingredients:

white radish
cucumber

The white radish is a high-energy vegetable ruled by Mars. Mars is the creator of strife. Sometimes the deity who rules a problem must be appeased in order for the problem to be alleviated. If you feel stressful in the evening and are having trouble relaxing, take a white radish and peel it as far down as you can. As you peel away the layers imagine the layers of stress being peeled away. Gather the peels and toss them into the garbage along with your problems. Peel the skin off a cucumber and slice it lengthwise in half, then cut across the middle to create four quarters. Salt the cucumber quarters and eat all four. Cucumber is ruled by the moon and is known as a vegetable of peace. Salt is a purifier and will also help to remove any excess stress. You should feel much more relaxed by the effects of this spell. Make sure to eat all four quarters as each one rules a different aspect of your being. The east relaxes your mind, the south tones down your drive, the west gives emotional peace, and the north brings physical relaxation.

HIGH ENERGY SPELL

Ingredients:

    cucumber
    white radish

Sometimes you come home so relaxed you could just sink right into bed. However, there are things to be done: places to go, people to see, children to feed, homework to be done. Whatever the case, I have found that by reversing the **Anti-Anxiety Spell** you can create excess energy to keep you from winding down before your work or play is done. Peel a cucumber until you hit the watery seeds. Turn it round and round with the peeler until you can peel no more. Imagine all your tiredness being absorbed as you hit the watery part of the cucumber. Gather up the peels and throw them out along with your tiredness. Cut a white radish into quarters and inhale the sharp scent as you do so. Eat as much of the radish as you can tolerate. The more you eat, the more energy you will receive. If you know you cannot finish it all, make sure to take at least a nibble from each quarter. The quarters represent the four elements. The element of air will give you mental alertness. The element of fire will give you willpower. The element of water gives emotional strength, and the element of earth gives you the physical strength to accomplish all you have to do.

GRAVEYARD SHIFT SPELL

Ingredients:

> **coffee beans**
> **mustard seeds**
> **brown, black, and red candles**
> **green olives or green cold-pressed olive oil**
> **garlic cloves**

This spell is to keep you awake when you have to work all night at the office. Fill a bowl with espresso coffee beans and mustard seeds and keep this on your desk or workspace. Coffee beans are ruled by Saturn and the sign of Capricorn, which represents hard work and focus. Mustard is both Mercurial and Martian and produces greater awareness, and sharpens and wakes up the mind. Mustard also produces speed to help you plow through your work. It is not necessary to eat these foods; you can simply sniff them in the bowl from time to time or run your fingers through the beans and seeds in the bowl whenever you need to gather more energy.

Brown candles are burned for staying power, black for concentration, and red for energy. Olives or olive oil purifies and grants longevity. This will help you get through the long haul of working through the wee hours. Also, the combination of olive and mustard helps to manage time. They will prevent you from feeling as though the time will never pass and will also prevent you from losing time and not accomplishing any work. The blend helps you to utilize your time in the most efficient way possible. Green olives or green olive oil also adds the element of prosperity, as time is money. Anoint all candle colors with green olive oil or light unanointed candles and snack on green olives as you work.

The final ingredient is garlic cloves, roasted or raw. It is said that the slaves in Egypt ate whole cloves of garlic while building the Great Pyramids. Eat one clove every three hours for stamina.

MIGUEL'S SPELL

Primero hay que saber sufrir / despues amar / despues partir,
y luego andar sin pensamiento . . .
Perfume de naranjo en flor / promesas vanas de un amor
que se escaparon con el viento . . .
—Homero Expósito

Ingredients:

persimmon
the leaves and fruit of an orange
cloves
a river or body of water in the west
mulberry jam
honeysuckle or any sweet melon

Miguel was dumped by Maria over twenty years ago, yet his grief is still as fresh as the perfume of orange blossoms on a summer's eve wind whispering through an orange grove in southern Florida. Miguel has accepted his fate. He does not want to love again. Miguel is not even able to stand up from bed more than two or three hours in a day. His nights are spent in mindless wandering around the city, trying to forget, yet clinging to the distant memory of Maria for all his soul is worth.

I met Miguel late one night in the paper products aisle of the supermarket. I heard a commotion two aisles down so I headed over to see what the trouble was. Miguel was being harassed by an overzealous stock clerk who had caught him red-handed opening a box of tissues to sob into. Miguel had no money to pay for the merchandise. I placed the open box of tissues in my shopping cart, flashed some green at the clerk to back him off, and looped my arm through the arm of the lost Miguel. He followed me down several aisles quite passively as if he were sleep-walking. I swiftly and quietly filled my cart with a persimmon, a beautiful orange with the stem and two leaves still attached, a bottle of whole cloves, mulberry jam, and another box of tissues, just in case things got out of hand. I paid for all the items and led Miguel out into a warm June night. We headed toward the Hudson River, which is on New York's west side. The west is the direction that rules the emotions, creativity, and dreams. I intended to transform Miguel's grief into something more creative. On the walk over, Miguel began to open up to me and revealed the source of his woe. He said after twenty years, he felt his suffering was complete, yet he knew no way to release it.

"I can help you, Miguel, not only to release it, but to transform it as well, into something worthy of the beauty of Maria and the majesty of your suffering." As we reached the river I sliced the persimmon in half, offered half to Miguel and tossed the other half as an offering into the river. Persimmons are ruled by Venus and the element of water. They are alleged to bring happiness. Persimmons are a tricky fruit, as they can be awfully bitter or wonderfully sweet. It is because of this quality that they are said to turn sorrow into joy. I chose a very soft persimmon to ensure its sweetness for Miguel. Next we took turns pushing cloves into the orange. As we did so, I wrapped the leaf of the orange around a clove and instructed

Miguel to chew on it. Cloves are known to be purifying and were used to comfort mourners. Combined with orange they enhance passion and renew the heart. Next I anointed the entire orange with mulberry jam. Miguel also placed a fingerful of jam under his tongue. Mulberry is sacred to Minerva, sacred Roman goddess of the arts. She is also associated with Athena, the Greek goddess, who was born of the head of Zeus. Miguel was already a man of passion and heart; I wanted to awaken his mind. After fully anointing the orange, Miguel held it between both hands and we prayed for a positive way for him to express his passion. Miguel tossed the orange high into the air and we watched it plop into the Hudson and make its way south. Miguel said he felt as if a great weight had been lifted from his shoulders. He lifted me up and we began to dance along the bank of the Hudson under the light of a full moon. I walked him home, and on the way, we passed a fence covered with honeysuckle. We each pulled a small flower and sucked the drop of honey from the delicate stem. Honeysuckle is the flower of wit and prose, sacred to the spirits of Mercury.*

Two days later, I received the most beautiful letter from Miguel, thanking me for my guidance and help. Two months later, he gave up the horrid railroad flat in Hell's Kitchen that he had been rotting away in and moved back to his native Uruguay. He has become a very successful and celebrated South American poet.

*If you cannot find honeysuckle, you may substitute any sweet melon. Do not eat the fruit, but extract juice from it and drink a few drops.

Intimate Evenings/Hot and Heavy Nights

STERN UND HIMMEL* SPELL

(for Jim)

Ingredients:

dark plums

Plums are ruled by Bacchus, which gives them the qualities of spontaneity and sex appeal. There is another mystical quality to the plum. If you look at a very dark plum, you will notice the little white dots or flecks, which make the plum reminiscent of a night sky filled with stars.

Eat plums with a partner for a romantic evening under the stars. You can also

*Estrella y cielo

eat plums alone to increase your star quality and sex appeal. As you take a bite make a wish upon a star.

Drink plum wine with a partner to increase the desire for each other. To find your way to seventh heaven, bathe in a tub of water with seven plums or seven cups of plum wine.

FLAMING LOVE SPELL

Ingredients:

firewood
a knife

This is a very simple yet quite effective spell to keep the desire eternally alive in a relationship. You will need a fireplace or an open campfire to perform the ritual. Please do not attempt to perform this spell in your oven or microwave.

You and your beloved must sit together by a warm fire. Once the fire is burning brightly, carve your initials together into a piece of wood. You should carve his or her initials and he or she should carve yours. Once the initials are carved, seal them with a kiss. You should kiss your lover's initials and your lover should kiss your initials. Throw the wood on the fire and kiss each other as it burns. Hold hands with fingers interlocked and gaze into the fire. Let your faces, hearts, and entire bodies be warmed by the heat of that flame. Make a wish for your passion for each other to last forever. Do not let the fire go out with this log. You must add at least three more logs before the fire can go out. If you drink a glass of wine in front of this fire, you will gain more spiritual or tantric wisdom about each other.

If you share a glass of beer in front of this fire, your relationship will be protected from negative and interfering influences. If you drink fresh-pressed apple cider in front of this fire, you will never be able to be unfaithful to each other.

It is said that spirits live in wood, and they often grant wishes to petitioners. The magical notion of carving lovers' names into trees is centuries old. The element of fire represents passion. Fire is also a powerful way to release magic. According to ancient legend, fire is the greatest gift ever given to humankind. I would argue that the gift of love sits right beside it!

OPIUM EVENING

Ingredients:

> **poppy seeds**
> **cardamom seeds**
> **papaya seeds**
> **pomegranate seeds**

The poppy and pomegranate are both surrounded with psychedelic and hallucinogenic mythology. Who can forget the image of Margaret Hamilton in *The Wizard of Oz* as she waved her broom over the poppy field. The pomegranate is the gateway to the underworld, visions, the unknown, the forbidden secrets of the occult. Papaya and cardamom are considered love drugs and magical opiates.

This spell is for a magical mystery tour of love. It is used to create a sensual and psychedelic night of love without the use of illegal drugs. Roast poppy seeds, shelled cardamom seeds, papaya seeds, and pomegranate seeds for fifteen minutes. Eat together with your partner or eat alone before a night of cruising.

SEXY NIGHTIE SPELL

(This spell is for those of you who spend a fortune in sexy lingerie while your partner still falls asleep without noticing.)

Ingredients:

coffee beans
loose tobacco
ginger
cinnamon
bay

Coffee beans and loose tobacco are used to wake your lover up. They are also believed to increase sexual performance and endurance. The combination of ginger, cinnamon, and bay is an old witch's formula known as Flaming Power or Flaming Desire. It is used to excite and arouse passion and sexual desire in your lover.

Grind fresh coffee beans, loose tobacco,* ginger, cinnamon sticks, and bay leaves to a fine powder. Sprinkle the powder under the mattress, kitchen table, or anywhere else that you would like to be ravaged in your lingerie.

In some difficult cases, the powder should be spread where the uninterested partner will be sure to walk barefoot. Once the powder touches the soles of his or her feet, passion is sure to be aroused.

*You can use pipe tobacco or empty out the contents of a rolled cigarette.

CAPTURE THE KNIGHT SPELL

Ingredients:

> **mace**
> **red candle**

Have you ever had a hot night of lovemaking ruined because your mind is focusing on the morning after? You can't even enjoy the pleasure your body is indulging in because your mind is thinking: "Will he still respect me in the morning? Will he call me next week? Will he still love me a year from now?" This spell is designed to shift your focus to the here and now as well as to reassure your fears about those gnawing questions. This spell is for use by heterosexual women or gay men only.

It is whispered in the Louisiana bayous that if a woman douches with the herb mace before making love to a man, she can hold him forever. Work this spell to hold a man forever or until you tire of him, whichever should occur first. The spell can only be performed seven to ten hours before you plan to have vaginal or anal intercourse with this man. The spell is quite effective when used to hold a boyfriend or husband you feel is about to stray or to turn a first-time encounter into more than a one-night stand. It can also be used on men with whom you have been engaging sexually to help create a strong, passionate, and loving commitment.

Because of health reasons, I cannot recommend douching with mace. It is possible that some people may have an allergic reaction to the herb. *Do so at your own risk.* The spell as I have designed it works as follows: On a Monday, Tuesday, or Friday evening at dusk, take a short red candle and rub with mace. Take a small clipping of your pubic hair and place underneath the candle. Burn the candle and stare into the flame. Chant: "Forever mine. You will love and pine after me forever. Forever mine." Allow the candle to burn halfway and then snuff it out by placing a dab of saliva between your right thumb and index finger. You must then consummate the act before the sun comes up. *Be sure that the man wears a condom.* Also be sure to procure the used condom afterward. On the following night, at dusk, turn the condom inside out and rub some of his semen onto the wick. Relight the candle and let it burn completely. Chant: "Come to me come to me forever and always be mine."

When the candle has extinguished itself, gather up the wax remains and shape into a heart. Carve both your initials into the heart. Keep in a safe place. If you ever need a booster ritual, take the wax heart out and sprinkle mace on top. Then sprinkle the mace from the heart into the shoes of the man or on a spot he is sure to walk across.

Note: If there is no residual wax left over once the candle burns, it means one of two things: You do not truly desire this man for keeps and your obsession will eventually die down, or the man will fall in love with you without witchcraft and the spell is not truly needed.

MOON-KISSED SPELLS

Ingredients:

> **figs**
> **peaches**
> **kumquats**

apples or cooked white rice
nutmeg
a bright full moon

Our society is very solar oriented. Everyone responds to a sun-kissed fruit or vegetable ripening in the sun. Sun worship still exists despite all kinds of warnings about skin cancer. Even in some circles of the occult, solar energy is considered more positive than lunar energy. For example, in the Tarot cards, the Sun Trump is believed to foretell happiness, health, and good fortune, whereas the Moon Trump is associated with danger and illusion. Lunar energy is considered to be feminine, and there are still many superstitions and fears surrounding women's power and mystery. These spells summon the more subtle powers of nature and shed a more positive light on the image of that long-maligned secondary orb.

Figs

This spell is most effective in creating a sexual undercurrent in your own aura, and to subconsciously influence others with your sex appeal. You will need a fresh or dried fig. It is here that using moonlight as opposed to sunlight becomes as different as night and day. To charge a fig with sunlight and then ingest it might be overkill (like wearing a loud red dress with everything hanging out). To charge a fig with moonlight and then eat it would create more cunning effects (wearing an elegant black frock with just a hint of garter showing). The fig in and of itself is a very powerful aphrodisiac and sexual attractant. To infuse it with moonlight will add sensuality, mystery, and style. To add sunlight would be like stripping it bare before it's ripened.

Hold a fig between your palms and raise your arms up to the heavens. Roll the fig around in your hands and let the full moonlight penetrate it from all sides. Eat the fig and visualize the moonlight entering your own body and aura.

Peaches

Perhaps you need to project your inner wisdom this evening? Hold a peach up to the full moon and let the peach absorb the light. Eat and reflect upon the light and fruit opening up your centers of knowledge and intelligence. This spell can also open the mind to receiving insights and to increase learning abilities (eat before studying all night for exams). The peach is prized for its longevity. Because the tree lives so long, it is believed to have acquired much wisdom.

Kumquats

The kumquat is used to attract luck and money. These small fruits are best charged by the light of the first sliver of the new moon. This way your luck and money will begin to grow. Charge on a full moon if you have a specific financial goal that you want to bring to fruition. You can eat the kumquats, or you may carry them in the pocket or handbag as a magical talisman. These talismans will only last until two days after the full moon. Then you must wait until the next new or full moon to create another. You can thank the talisman and dispose of it properly.

Apples

An apple sprinkled with nutmeg, charged by the light of the full moon, and shared by lovers can strengthen a relationship and make the couple more intuitively aware of each other's needs. Apples are used to find and preserve true love. Nutmeg increases the psychic vibrations and fine-tunes spiritual and tantric awareness. You can also hold a bowl of cooked white rice sprinkled with nutmeg under the light of the full moon. Rice is believed to bind the souls of lovers. Eat the bowl of rice with your partner under the full moon.

ROMANCE RICE BALLS

Ingredients:

**sushi rice and jasmine rice
bay leaves
salt
cardamom
corn
Parmesan cheese
shallots
tomato
basil
rosemary
pure butter and olive oil**

peas
thyme
bread crumbs
garlic (optional)
chili powder
honey
egg yolks

This recipe is designed to bring true love and romance into your life. If you are already married or in a serious relationship, prepare and eat the rice balls on a full moon to bring out the full potential of a relationship. If you are in a new relationship, just started dating, or are ready and willing to meet someone new, prepare and eat on a new moon. If you are having serious problems in a relationship, or if you are experiencing serious blocks to meeting someone new, prepare and eat on the waning moon. If you are in a relationship, you must eat with your partner. If you are alone, eat one rice ball and leave one outside under a tree as a symbolic offering to your new mate. Please pick up the offering when you are done eating. Bring it home and place it in a dish on a table until morning. Then you may dispose of it.*

Begin by cooking a highly starched rice, as you want the rice to be sticky. Sushi rice is recommended. Mix the sushi rice with jasmine rice as jasmine is a flower of love. Mix three bay leaves and three pinches of salt into the rice water. Bay and salt will purify and protect a love. Also add seven shelled and crushed cardamom seeds to flavor the rice. Cardamom adds passion. Add corn niblets as rice is cooking

---

*It is important not to leave the rice ball unattended. It is meant only as a symbolic offering. You do not want a wild dingo or local wino to eat your offering and then fall madly in love with you.

or when it's almost done. The corn will cook from steam. Add Parmesan cheese, stir, and let cool. While the rice is cooling, sauté shallots, tomatoes, basil, rosemary, and thyme in a pan with pure butter, pure olive oil, and a teaspoon of honey. (You may also add two cloves of garlic to increase fertility in the relationship.) After tomatoes soften, smash them to release water. Cover and simmer until water is absorbed. Mix together with cooked rice after removing bay leaves.

Beat two egg yolks and mix with bread crumbs. Add a pinch of chili powder to the bread crumbs to bring a hot romance. To make the rice balls, take some rice in your hand and press some peas in the middle; add more rice on top of peas and roll into a ball. Make layers so that peas are in the center. Roll the ball in the egg yolk and bread crumbs. Cook in olive oil with basil and rosemary. Roll around in pan until brown. Eat under the moon and stars if possible.

Shallots are believed to delicately cleanse and open the chakras. It is important to be open to give and receive love. Shallots are also believed to get rid of misfortune. Basil is an herb sacred to Mars, god of sex, and tomatoes are sacred to Venus, goddess of love. Corn is a fertility food. It can bring grounding, fertility, or nurturing to a relationship. Peas are sacred to Venus and eaten to attract beauty, love, and harmony into life. Bread is a food of sustenance and no one can survive without love. The bread crumbs also serve as a symbolic path so that you will not lose your way in love. Olive oil brings spiritual awakenings and is also known as a love oil. It can enhance the romance with a spiritual element. The Chinese lore around rice is very extensive. It is believed that two people can bind their souls together during the nuptial vows by sharing a bowl of rice. Western customs dictate throwing rice at the newlyweds to bless the union. Cheese and butter are nurturing foods because they are ruled by the moon and binding foods because they are also ruled by Saturn. Rosemary and thyme are used for fidelity and enhance a relationship with thoughtfulness and respect. Honey is used to sweeten and bless the life of the relationship, and eggs bring constant renewal to your vows.

DREAM LOVER SPELL

Ingredients:

gardenia
poppy
rose

Gardenia represents the power principle in love. Rose opens the heart. A nocturnal flower, poppy is said to have strong magical influence during the night hours. It can produce a dreamy state, or affect the nature of dreams, and also produce hypnotic effects. Combined with rose and gardenia it can lure and attract on a deep subconscious level.

Witches will traditionally combine the essential oils or dried flowers of these three ingredients. The oil can be worn as a perfume, rubbed on candles, or burned as liquid incense. The dried flowers can be added to a bath or burned as incense. The supermarket version can be designed by purchasing scented soaps of gardenia and rose. Soften the soaps in hot water and then roll them in poppy seeds. You can then use the soaps to take a magical bath. This bath should be taken to produce a dreamy night in bed with the one you love.

A second method of working the spell requires one candle scented with rose and one scented with gardenia. Place the candles so that they are touching each other and surround them in a circle of poppy seeds. Burn to make someone dream of you the morning after your night out. The candles can also be used to bring you to mind while the person is out with someone else.

To create a sensual mood within a space, spray rose and gardenia air fresheners around the room and serve poppy seed cakes. If you can obtain dried rose and gardenia petals, mix them in a bowl with poppy seeds and leave out as a potpourri. You can also carry the dried potion in a purse or pocket to attract that dreamy someone.

BOTTICELLI AND THE BROTHEL

Ingredients:

graven images or paper ones

While in a mega supermarket one afternoon, my eye began to notice a plethora of antiquated pagan images, which now seem to inundate modern culture by way of advertising. Ancient gods and goddesses beckoning us to buy produce, chocolates, and grain. Greeting cards and candles bearing the likeness of Michelangelo's David and Botticelli's Venus on the half shell. In one fish market, the Lady's image was even used to sell clams.

Witches and pagans constantly use graven images on their altars and in magic spells. Although we do not believe that these images are actually the god and goddess, we do believe these images symbolize divine power and can be used as conduits to draw on that energy, much the same as a house of worship serves as a conduit between the prayers of humanity and the ears of God, saints, or angels. A box of cornstarch with the image of Ceres sitting on the grocer's shelf is not likely to answer your prayers. However, purchasing that box, taking it home, cutting out the image, and placing it upon an altar adorned with other representations of this goddess and her powers is most likely to become a medium for magical energy. My personal preference is to adorn my altar with ancient statuary. However, there are many new age techniques of creative visualization that have proven quite effective. Some involve cutting out images from magazines, newspapers, box tops, and books to illustrate your desires or to invoke divine inspiration into your life. The power is not in the price of the thing but rather in the energy with which you adorn it.

Case in point: There is a very famous *puuf** located on a side street just off the Ku'damm, Berlin's most lively thoroughfare. It is so famous that one can hail a taxi anywhere in Berlin, mention the name of the proprietor of the house, and the driver will know the exact location of your destination. My cousin, Willie, who frequents this house, told me of a most curious custom practiced in the bordello. The ground floor of this house is broken up into three sitting rooms equipped with bars, divans, soft lighting, red velvet walls, and gold lamé ceilings from which hang ornate chandeliers. It is here that the men unwind, order drinks, and socialize with the girls. In the back of the ground floor is a large kitchen complete with an Italian chef, who makes sure that the girls have enough food in their stomachs to absorb all the alcohol that is consumed during the course of an evening. Off of the kitchen is the office of the Madam, Lady Lena. It is here that she sits upon a large throne surrounded by a video security system so that she can monitor the goings on in the house. There are also several private rooms on the ground floor, each with a different theme. Willie is very fond of a particular room downstairs; it is a rococo replica of Marie Antoinette's bedroom in Versailles, with the added touch of a 1960s water bed. Willie has another favorite room upstairs, which I will hold off from describing, because it is the journey up the stairs of the bordello that leads to this curious custom that I set out to describe.

The centerpiece of the ground floor is the spiral staircase leading up to the private rooms of the house. The staircase is visible from each of the main bars. It is covered

---

*brothel. By the way, they are legal in Germany.

in plush red carpeting with tiny rows of lights set into each step. To the left of the staircase is a balcony upon which rests a large statue of Botticelli's Venus. The statue is bathed in red light emanating from a beautiful antique lamp. The lamp hangs on the wall, next to the shoulder of the statue.* During the course of an evening those coming up and down the staircase will stop and linger by the statue. They will kiss the three fingers (index, pointer, and ring) of their right hands and then rub those fingers against the vagina of the Venus while making a wish. According to Willie, all these wishes come true.

Cousin Wilheim is what is known as a poor little rich boy, or a man of title without means. His father had been a very wealthy and philanthropic man. He left everything to Willie, who went through his entire inheritance in Monaco within three months after receiving it. (Unfortunately, Uncle Wolfgang did not believe in trust funds.) Luckily for Willie, his father's reputation lives on and sometimes Willie can bank on it. For instance, Lady Lena, whose heart (and the diamond chip in her front tooth) shine brighter than all the gold in Fort Knox, and whose bank account is worth ten times that, will never forget Uncle Wolfgang. His business alone funded her castle in Poland and one of her three helicopters. Willie was thirteen years old when he first visited the brothel. His father brought him there to celebrate his coming into manhood, and it was Lady Lena herself who unsheathed him of his virginity. Willie is always welcome at Lady Lena's and always gets a meal, a bottle, and a girl on the house. Unlike the rest of the male clientele, Willie knows all the gossip of the house, and at times he is even treated as one of the girls. It is due to this situation that I became privy to the magical goings on that occurred on a particular Friday night.

---

*Obviously this idol is being tended to, as red is the color of Venus and the lamp is one of her magical tools.

It was a full moon in December. The spirit of Christmas was in the air and Yuletide cheer abounded in the house. Someone was playing the piano and singing Brecht. Girls in red satin, black silk, feather boas, corsets, and straps filtered in and out. Willie had been there since eighteen hundred hours, and it was now on the heels of the witching hour. He was bored with the usual fare and wandered into the kitchen for something al dente. Willie found Eva, his favorite courtesan, crying her eyes out. It seems she had fallen in love with *ein Junger Seemann.** The sailor had proposed marriage, but when Eva declined, he decided to head back out to sea on a long and indefinite journey. Eva had reconsidered and was desperate to catch her lover before he vanished forever on the ocean's foam.

"Maybe I can help," said Willie.

All at once, Lady Lena, with her long black leonine mane of curls, swung through the kitchen doors bellowing: "*Spiel nicht die beleidigte Leberwurst!*"**

"Why can't she go?" asked Willie.

"*Herr Johann kommt. Er ist nicht mit Gold zu bezahlen und Eva ist mit allen Wassern gewaschen!*"† With that final word, Lady Lena stormed out of the kitchen.

Herr Johann was a relatively easy mark. He spent most of his money on alcohol. He could sit and drink with a girl for hours and hours. He loved to ask them questions about their lives. By the time it came down to the actual business of the brothel, Herr Johann had usually passed out cold. Eva began to sob even harder as she realized that this enchanted evening had no end in sight.

---

*a young sailor
**"*Don't play with the baked Liverwurst!*" No, actually it means, "*Stop acting the prima donna!*"
†Herr Johann, my most important client, is on his way and Eva is his favorite trick!

"Eva, Eva, don't cry. Come upstairs with me. I have an idea." said Willie, beginning to imagine a cure for his ennui.

Eva tearfully followed him out of the kitchen. The office door was ajar, and as they passed by the monarch of the house, Willie popped his head in and said with a wink, "Just thought I'd warm her up for Johann."

Lena waved them away and stuck her head back in her accounting books. As they mounted the stairs Willie and Eva both paused to kiss the mound of Venus.

"Dear goddess of good sailing and the ocean, bestower of the bridal chamber—get me to Hamburg and help me reach my lover's ship on time. Oh sustainer of the side glancers—please let Lena look the other way. This is my wish," whispered Eva through her tears.

Willie's wish went something like this: "Oh slayer of men and lover of laughter; goddess of aphrodisiacs and cosmetics, mother of Hermaphrodite—I wish to be a beautiful woman."

"Poof!" said Willie as he dragged Eva down the hall to his favorite room. It was actually one big walk-in closet filled with enough dresses and shoes to turn Imelda Marcos green with envy. There was a large vanity filled with cosmetics. The king-sized bed was shaped like a stiletto heel and draped with lion skins. Willie shed his clothes, hopped onto the bed, and began applying makeup. Eva, catching on, rummaged through the rack and found the perfect outfit. She helped Willie transform, and together they took some thick rope from the bondage wardrobe and tied it to the balcony. Willie touched up his lipstick while Eva slid down the rope and hightailed it to Hamburg. At that point, Lady Lena decided to surf through the channels of her security television. She spied a strange and striking, yet curiously familiar woman powdering her nose while unknotting a rope from the balcony. The madam huffed and puffed up the stairs and goose-stepped into the room.

"Was man sich eingebrockt hat, das muß man auch auslöffeln," * hissed Lady Lena.

Willie obediently assumed a seductive pose on the bed. Lady Lena marched down the stairs and came to a halt in front of the statue as she spied Herr Johann enter the establishment. She inserted three fingers into her bosom (where she keeps her cash), kissed them, and prayed: *"Oh meine Lieblings Göttin . . . die Sache hat einen Haken. Hilf mir, bitte. Zeig mir das geld."* **

She smiled coyly at Herr Johann and beckoned him upstairs, saying:

"Begeben Sie sich in die Höhle des Löwen und sehen Sie was dort lauert." †

Herr Johann cocked his head and slowly rose from the bar.

"Wieviel flaschen Champagne?" ‡ asked Lady Lena.

"Just one," he said smiling. "I think I'd like to stay up this evening."

Herr Johann eagerly ascended the stairs and kissed the mound, saying: "Oh goddess of the headland and beautiful backside, giver of joy and soother of genitals—make this a night unlike any other night!

Well, Lady Lena got paid handsomely for the evening. Herr Johann was delighted and never stops speaking of it. Eva got married and presently works only part-time. Willie—well, Wilheim is now very careful about what he wishes for.

---

*"You've made your bed. Now lie in it."

**"Oh dearest Goddess of success and bountiful ocean, whose holy weapons are the girdle and necklace (here she touches her bosom once again); She who joins; She who contrives; persuasive Lady; bringer of luck to the courtesan—Help me. Please let Herr Johann pay his usual rate and not discover the hook in the bait!"

†"Step into the lion's den and see what lurks there."

‡How many bottles of champagne?

BIBLIOGRAPHY

Anderson, James. *Dictionary of Opera and Operetta*. Britain: Richard Clay Ltd., 1989.

Crowley, Aleister. *777*. York Beach, Maine: Samuel Weiser, Inc., 1996.

Cunningham, Scott. *The Magic in Food*. St. Paul, MN: Llewellyn Pub., 1990.

Farrar, Janet, and Stewart Farrar. *The Witches' God*. Custer, Washington: Phoenix Publishing, Inc., 1989.

Farrar, Janet, and Stewart Farrar. *The Witches' Goddess*. Custer, Washington: Phoenix Publishing, Inc., 1995.

Guirand, Felix, ed. *New Larousse Encyclopedia of Mythology*. Hong Kong: The Hamlyn Publishing Group Ltd., 1972.

Hand, Robert. *Planets in Transit*. Atglen, PA: Whitford Press, 1976.

Hand, Wayland D., Anna Cassetta, and Sondra B. Theiderman, eds. *Popular Beliefs and Superstitions: A Compendium of American Folklore*. Boston: G.K. Hall, 1981.

Holland, Jack. *The Real Guide Berlin*. New York: Prentice Hall Press, 1990.

Jensen, Bernard. *Blending Magic*. Solana Beach, CA: Bernard Jensen Products.

Jim, Papa. *Papa Jim Magical Herb Book*. San Antonio, TX: 1985.

Leach, Maria, ed. *Funk & Wagnalls Standard Dictionary of Folklore, Mythology, and Legend*. San Francisco: Harper & Row, 1984.

Lupson, J.P. *Sprachführer zu Deutschen Idiomen*. Chicago, IL: Passport Books, 1995.

Mariechild, Diane. *Mother Wit*. Freedom, CA: The Crossing Press, 1981.

Mathers, S. Liddell MacGregor, trans. *The Goetia: The Lesser Key of Solomon the King*. York Beach, ME: Samuel Weiser Inc., 1997.

Mathers, S. Liddell MacGregor, trans. *The Key of Solomon the King*. York Beach, ME: Samuel Weiser Inc., 1989.

Morgan, Chris. *Zukunfts—deutung*. London: Quintet Publishing Ltd., 1992.

Panati, Charles. *Panati's Extraordinary Origins of Everyday Things*. New York: Harper & Row, 1987.

Radzinsky, Edvard. *The Last Tsar*. New York: Doubleday, 1992.

Riva, Anna. *Golden Secrets of Mystic Oils*. Los Angeles, CA: International Imports, 1990.

Riva, Anna. *The Modern Herbal Spellbook*. Los Angeles, CA: International Imports, 1974.

Rogers, Kasey. *The Bewitched Cookbook: Magic in the Kitchen*. New York: Kensington Books, 1996.

Rose, Donna. *The Magic of Herbs*. Hialeah, FL: Mi-World Pub. Co., 1978.

Rose, Donna. *The Magic of Oils*. Hialeah, FL: Mi-World Pub. Co., 1978.

Rose, H.J. *A Handbook of Greek Mythology*. New York: Penguin Books, 1991.

Rose, Jeanee. *Jeanee Rose's Herbal Guide to Food*. Berkeley, CA: North Atlantic Books, 1989.

de Sebastian, Isabel, ed. *Tango: La Posta Del Tango En*. New York: Tango World Ltd., 1997.

Slater, Herman, ed. *The Magical Formulary*. New York: Magickal Childe Pub. Inc., 1981.

Tannahill, Reay. *Food in History*. New York: Stein & Day, 1973.

Telesco, Patricia. *A Kitchen Witch's Cookbook*. St. Paul, MN: Llewellyn Publications, 1994.

Walker, Barbara. *Woman's Encyclopedia of Myths and Secrets*. San Francisco: Harper & Row, 1983.

Walker, Barbara. *Woman's Encyclopedia of Symbols and Sacred Objects*. San Francisco: HarperCollins, 1988.

Wasserman, James. *Art and Symbols of the Occult*. Rochester, NY: Destiny Books, 1993.

Wedeck, Harry, and Baskin, Wade. *Dictionary of Pagan Religions*. NJ: The Citadel Press, 1973.

Woodroffe, Sir John. *Hymns to the Goddess and Hymn to Kali*. Wilmot, WI: Lotus Light Publications, 1981.